ALEXI
LOVE AND WAR THROUGH TIME

BOOK 1
Demons from Hell-A Reign of Terror

CHARLES WALKER

authorHOUSE®

AuthorHouse™ LLC
1663 Liberty Drive
Bloomington, IN 47403
www.authorhouse.com
Phone: 1-800-839-8640

Published by AuthorHouse 06/12/2014

ISBN: 978-1-4969-1593-1 (sc)
ISBN: 978-1-4969-1592-4 (e)

CONTENTS

Chapter 1

Finding Alexi

Until my early teens, whenever I had to explain my actions for something that got me in trouble, I would stall by saying,

"I don't know where to begin."

Nana would respond in her best scolding voice, "Start at the beginning."

Here, the problem is there's more than one beginning. Maybe I should start when I met Alexi, since this story is about him.

I'm a journalist working for a magazine conglomerate, I write feature stories on culture, travel, and people of interest. Except when my publisher decides there's something deserving of my special talents, which happened at the end of October. I met Alexi in late December that same year.

At twenty-five I've been published more than many writers in their mid-thirties, according to my boss at least. He gave me this assignment to get my feet wet, as he put it, as a journalist in the field. Lately, rumors of vampire activity in the Carpathian Mountains, between the Czech Republic and Slovakia, was much discussed, but no reliable verification available.

My mission was to decide whether this was a ploy to attract tourists, or a maniac believing himself to be heir to the great 'Vlad the Impaler', aka 'Count Dracula', hence, Prague.

Nut cases are not my specialty, but I gladly accepted the all-expense-paid trip to the Czech Republic for up to a year. My publishers expected me to write weekly articles about other stories of interest; such as travelogues with accompanying photographs, and historical facts and fictions according to the local populace.

They especially wanted investigation in the Carpathian's small villages where the rumors reputedly started, where else? The people there needed tourist dollars, desperately as I was about to discover.

Arriving in Prague early on December 28, I went directly to the Hotel Majestic, which lives up to its name; a recently renovated structure built about 1920, it had escaped WWII's destruction. Its facade was impressive, and it truly was majestic, 12-floors of opulent grandeur from an era when Art Deco was in serious competition with the Elizabethan style.

Humanity is the winner of their ever greater innovations and excesses, with sculptured panels, also structural elements of the facade, and turrets, not the same as those on a castle, but seeming to hold up the floors above.

The total effect was that of a building carved from a gigantic block of granite, reminiscent of Egyptian monuments that make a person wonder how they could have built on such a colossal scale.

The impressive interior eclipsed the exterior; opposite the huge brass framed glass entry doors sat a massive reception desk. The marble front and top matched the wainscoting, and floor of the lobby, a sand colored marble with red streaks, a stunning display of Masonic artistry.

Making a complimentary impression of beauty and luxury was the furniture; sofas, chairs, tables, lamps, and other accouterments, which surpassed the magnificent marble work and color. The octagonal coffered ceiling completed the picture.

At either end of the 100-foot lobby a curved staircase with ornate brass balusters wound gently up to a mezzanine above the reception desk, overlooking the lobby. A bar, a smaller version of the reception desk, held court over a cozy and warm area with twenty or so small tables surrounded by plush gold velvet chairs.

A railing matching the ornate balustrade of the stairs fronted the mezzanine. Off to the side of the bar a small stage area and dance floor gave the intimacy that most likely existed in the twenties.

After checking in and unpacking some of my luggage, I inquired at the desk for an interpreter and guide. The hotel employees weren't very helpful, although they spoke passable English, they couldn't recommend anybody to translate.

The day was balmy for so late in December, around 60-degrees Fahrenheit, so I took a relaxing stroll in the park next to the hotel. Many young people were jogging, strolling, reading, and huddling in groups talking, taking advantage of the mild weather.

Sitting on a vacant bench unwinding after the long trip, a slightly effeminate, very pretty, young man approached the bench carrying a video-camera. He gestured as if asking permission to join me on the bench, I had no objection, and he sat down.

Speaking to me in Czech, he quickly understood he was getting nowhere. I explained in English that I was a visitor, and spoke no Czech. He spoke garbled English, and after several repetitions we began to understand each other.

By his own tortured words, he was a pornographer. He haunted the park paying young men to drop their shorts, videotaping them in different states of arousal. He offered me 2,000 crowns, approximately $100, to bare my penis for him to videotape because I looked like a movie star. He said I would make a very popular porn star, and much more money than 2,000 crowns.

With my refusal I indicated I was familiar with this gay-porn genre, and I was gay myself. With an annoyed attitude he informed me he wanted straight boys for his videos, and rose to leave.

I asked him to sit for a moment, and explained that I needed someone who spoke English well enough to translate for me, and did he know anybody who may be willing to take the job? After a few minutes thought he said,

"Yes, but he is not gay."

I replied that I wasn't looking for someone gay, just someone to translate. His name was Alexi Duburk, Electrical Engineering student at the University of Prague, just across the park.

Fortunately, school was still in session making up for time lost in the early fall, extreme heat had created electrical failures and classes were canceled. I went immediately to the Dean of Students office, and inquired about Alexi Duburk, explaining as best I could why I was looking for him.

After cajoling the young lady in charge, she told me he was about to begin New Year's break, and would be dismissed very soon. She gave me directions and a cardboard sign with his name on it. I nearly missed him.

Students were leaving as I approached the building; he was just coming down the steps. Noticing my sign he affirmed in Czech that he was Alexi Duburk, and asked why I was looking for him?

I could barely think, let alone answer. Talk about movie stars, this guy was the man described in gay novels as Adonis. I felt my stomach dropping around my knees, and concluded I had little or no chance of working with this beauty. Sometimes our intuitions are wrong, and gut feelings not entirely reliable. I managed to stammer,

"You speak English, right?"

His manner immediately softened, and he replied in English as perfect as mine,

"Yes I do and you're an American, New York if I'm not mistaken."

"I'm Carl Wellsey," I said as I held out my hand, "And you're right, I'm a New Yorker, how did you know that here in Prague?

He chuckled and teasingly said, "Got you wondering if I'm clairvoyant don't I?"

"Something like that, but you sound like a New Yorker too, what's the story?"

"My mother was an American, a New Yorker; she's a Czech now, but insisted I learn to speak English since I was old enough to talk."

His relaxed demeanor put me at ease, and I suggested we go somewhere to talk about a job as translator.

We found a small café a block from the university, ordered espressos, and I began,

"How familiar are you with the Czech Carpathian Mountains?"

"I grew up there, in Brno, Moravia about 40-kilometers from Hodonin, the largest town in the actual mountains. It's a gateway town; just small villages from there until you get to Poland or Slovakia, a tough trip through the mountains."

"Why do you want to go there? There's only scenery and peasants still living in the fourteenth-century, accessed by terrible roads with drop-offs that make you dizzy."

"My publisher wants me to investigate rumors of Vampire activity in the mountains that has not been confirmed or denied, have you heard anything of that nature?"

"Yes, it's all people talk about in Brno, the mountain people are very superstitious. A newlywed couple visiting a village far up in the mountains in late October disappeared. When their bodies were found by hunters last month, it appeared they had been drained of all their blood, how they determined that I don't know."

"The bodies were pretty badly chewed; animals aren't going to bypass a meal like that. Vampires make a much more intriguing explanation, though."

"Have the authorities investigated?" I asked, getting interested.

"No, they don't want the local populace to think it was anything but a case of two people getting lost and dying of exposure in frigid temperatures. So they removed the bodies, or what was left of them, back to Prague for autopsies, and that's the last we've heard from the authorities."

"Is there a way we could get a copy of the autopsy reports?"

"My mother is an MD and my father is a psychiatrist, they lived in Prague for years before I was born and know half the people it seems."

"They might be able to help you, but let me warn you, the authorities aren't going to like you stirring up the mountain clans. They're hard enough to handle when there's no controversy, get them riled, and you'll have mobs with torches and pitchforks marching on the castle."

"Whose castle is that?" I asked, suddenly very interested in the reason for my assignment, not just an all-expense-paid vacation.

"It's just the ruins of a castle," he replied, "The government thought it would be a good idea to clean up the area so tourists could safely visit this supposed hideout of 'Vlad the Impaler', where he fled to when his throne was usurped by his son."

"The Carpathians were then part of Romania, today that area is Czech, and Slovakian, the borders have changed so many times over the centuries that no one is positive who controlled what. The government started this vampire nonsense as a tourist magnet, it worked, and maybe it will work again."

This had the makings of a story with all the elements of a human interest thriller; two gruesome deaths, vampires, government chicanery and cover-up, locals scared witless, and fearless investigators solving the mystery.

Wellll, maybe not so fearless, there's still a vestige of our prehistoric fear of monsters and the supernatural that gives us pause. However exciting the prospect of exploring the ruins of a vampire's castle, caution is recommended.

Alexi was perfect for a guide and translator; I had to convince him to work with me. Explaining my assignment and the part he would play in it, I asked,

"What do you think a translator gets per day here in Prague?"

"Probably 2, 000 to 4,000-crowns, Prague is expensive compared to the rest of the Czech Republic, but that's only a guess," he said with a little grin, "I wouldn't need that much, though."

He wants to do it I thought, he's as intrigued by this as I am, so reel him in with an offer he can't refuse.

"I'll pay you 3,000-crowns a day or $150 American, whichever you want, all-expenses-paid, and a car when traveling. Cars in Prague are weapons driven with extreme aggressiveness, so you'll have to drive; I'm not that courageous yet. You'll have a private room when we're on the road more than one day, meals included. What do you think? We can negotiate if you want something else."

"That sounds very generous, I'm tempted to accept your offer, but I'd like to know more about what you expect of me," he replied with a poorly disguised attempt to not appear too eager, "Could you explain what I do when we're not on the road?"

"We would visit areas of historic and cultural interest, interviewing, and recording local people. We videotape the areas we've targeted, translate the recordings, and arrange all our information into a cogent picture of life in that area," I explained,

"Then I'll write a travelogue or a feature story, it doesn't have to be specifically tailored, they publish many magazines from fashion, to food, to guns, and way beyond. So it's easier than I make it sound. How about it? Are you interested?"

"Yes, very interested," he said, "The first part made me want to leave for the mountains today, the second part, although not as exciting, piqued my interest, and doesn't sound onerous at all. Is that it, no other requirements?"

"That's it for the job, but there's one more thing you have to know; I'm gay."

Alexi stiffened like a stone statue.

"I don't think this will work," he angrily replied through clenched teeth, "I'm straight, and I have no interest in gay people or their lifestyle, I'm sorry I wasted your time."

"I expected that reaction, Alexi, please hear me out before you go charging out the door," I pleaded, using the most persuasive voice I could muster. He sat back in his chair, "I told you that because I didn't want you to discover the fact on your own, and think I was trying to involve you in something you don't want to be involved in."

"I'm not looking for a gay partner or someone to toy with. I'm dedicated to the job at hand, and I promise you my hands off policy, sex will not be spoken of, no lewd comments, no suggestive leers, no double entendres, and no comparisons to anything homosexual. If I fail on any one of these I will give you a full 2-weeks' pay and we'll part with no animosity."

"Can I trust you to do that?" he asked, "What guarantee do I have that when we're on the road you wouldn't try something, when we're miles away from home?"

"It's the middle of winter, we're not going anywhere for a few months, and I'll do my utmost until then to earn your trust and respect. I give you my word, and that is not given lightly."

He hesitated a moment and said, "How about we give it a trial run for a couple of weeks, then decide whether I trust you, and if you can stomach my homophobia?"

"It's a deal," I replied, as we self consciously shook hands. I tried to suppress the thrill touching his hand caused.

Later in my hotel room I mulled over in my mind the events of the last few hours; the park, the video guy, the university, our chat in the café, and his reaction to my confession. Something didn't quite feel right, and I analyzed it several times from different perspectives.

A question came to mind, how did the pornographer know Alexi? His name, his school, his major, and mostly, how did he know Alexi was in school today? The porn guy was gay, and Alexi had a severe case of homophobia, so what possible connection could exist between such disparate personalities? I was determined to unravel the mystery.

A troubled night wrestling with the porno guy mystery ensued, and by morning I was no closer to an answer than I was the night before. My suspicion was that Alexi and porno guy had an encounter that must have been more than casual for porno guy to know so much about Alexi.

Porno guy didn't seem to have a problem with Alexi; he actually was very generous to recommend him for a job. On the other hand, Alexi's homophobia would preclude him from being a best bud of porno man, unless he recently became homophobic.

Off on that tangent, all manner of scenarios presented themselves; it had to be a sexual contact, porno guy told me himself that he paid young guys, for what, God only knows. Whatever the outcome of the encounter, the porno guy seems to have emerged satisfied or at least not with his feathers ruffled. Otherwise would he have so readily been Alexi's advocate?

Conversely, could porno guy be blackmailing Alexi? After a successful encounter he paid Alexi, and wanted to shoot more videos. When Alexi balked at that idea, he threatened him with exposure, and got him to agree to another video.

Conjecture to be sure, but what other possible situation could fit all the coincidental facts I had at my disposal. I considered asking him about it at a latter date, and rejected that as a violation of my promise, so I'd have to become a detective and watch for clues.

Later, after having done my daily ablutions, and eaten my breakfast, I called Alexi; I experienced the same thrill as the day before.

He answered his phone with a cheerful "Good morning Carl, I was expecting you to call this morning. I figured you would probably want to set up a plan of action."

He surprised me, but truth be told, I had a good feeling that he wasn't so intractable that it would preclude us from working together.

"You're perceptive *and* clairvoyant I see; do you suppose we could use these talents in our little endeavor? I'd like to get together for a while today if you're not busy, for exactly the reasons you stated. I also want to pick your brain for possible subjects that we could investigate and develop into feature articles."

"I told you I expected this, so I'm available as long as you need me. I'll meet you at your hotel if you don't mind, I've never been in the hotel, and I'd love to see it, okay?"

"Yes, of course, let's see how compatible we are on architecture, we can spend a few minutes discussing the finer points of Art Deco architecture versus modern glass boxes. Come over whenever you're ready. Call me and I'll come down to the lobby, I can't wait to see your reaction to the obscene luxury down there."

"I'm in the park now, is 5-minutes too soon?"

"No, I'll head downstairs now, see you in five."

He's still eager to do this I thought, this still might work out, I hope! With that thought in my head, I headed for the lobby.

We got to the huge doors at the same time; I was amazed how good it felt to see him again, maybe because he's so easy to look at. I mentally rapped my knuckles for thinking along those lines; it would only cause me trouble and heartache if I continued. So I wore my most winning smile and shook his hand, he was warm, affable, and totally blown away by the hotel lobby.

"How long do you think it took to make this floor look like one continuous block of marble? There's not one place on this whole floor where a seam of red is cut off."

He's a quick study, I thought, less than 1-minute in the hotel, and he's already noticed the immaculate workmanship with the marble. Turning around slowly several times he took in the opulence with a look of someone gazing at the Mona Lisa. He obviously appreciated beauty; his eyes were shining as brightly as spotlights.

We walked up one of the curved stairs, strolled through the bar, and down the opposite stairs; to say the lobby impressed him is a gross understatement.

"It's hard to believe people actually live like this." He whispered, "You were right when you called it obscene luxury. It's beautiful, but so unnecessary, how many people starved while this was being built?"

"Aha! You also have a social conscience, I'm getting to like you more all the time, maybe we're more alike than we realize. Let's leave this mausoleum and brainstorm for a while."

"Yeah, this place is a little overwhelming. Is it me, or does this place make you feel like a small person?" he asked, "I feel like an ant in a very large marble box."

"That's what the designer was aiming for, the bigger and grander you could build, the more prestige you accrued and the more money you made. The amount of wealth wasted to build this fantastic building was obscene, but I take the same view of the cathedrals at Rheims, Chartres, and Notre-Dam."

"All that wealth built monuments to God while tens of thousands of people were starving and dying. The religious fanatics were oblivious of their suffering, claiming the greater glory was to build more, and the poor be damned."

Alexi was staring at me with a strange look on his face, "Do you suppose you and I are twins separated at birth?"

We laughed and snickered at his wise-crack for 10-minutes, the ice was broken.

Alexi should prove a valuable asset to our enterprise. He knew all the recent happenings in Prague; political-good, and corrupt, social events, famous people in the news, disasters, crime, and even statistics on the bizarre weather Eastern Europe was experiencing. We had a real smorgasbord of subjects to submit to the publishers.

By noon, after creating a priority list of events that would generate interest, we had enough on our list to last through the winter. At lunch in a downtown Bistro Alexi introduced me to Czech food, fairly spicy, but not hot spicy, it was delicious, and my estimation of him went up another notch.

We spent 2-hours visiting points of interest downtown, talking together as if we had known each other for years. He asked me if I worked out, I told him I did, 4-days a week. He invited me to his gym and showed me his routine, which seemed much more effective than mine.

Alexi and I are about the same weight, I'm 165-pounds he's 5-pounds heavier, but it's probably muscle mass. I'm 6-foot, so is he, he's physically fit with a not too sculpted body, me too. His crack about twins now didn't seem so funny. Our main statistical difference is age, I'm 3-years older than Alexi, but he kiddingly told me I could pass for twenty-four.

Before dinner we had a glass of wine at the dining-room bar, it was December 29, almost New Years. I started to get depressed thinking I'd be alone. Nana was always there, we would celebrate New Years at midnight, toast each other with a glass of champagne, and say goodnight.

When I was younger we would go see the fireworks, and it never bothered me that I had no one else to celebrate with. However, this year I didn't even have Nana, and I thought how lonely we would be 2-nights hence. Alexi must have noticed my morose mood.

"What are you doing on New Year's Eve?" he inquired, "Going to the street cleaner's ball?"

I laughed and asked, "What's a street cleaner's ball?"

"That's for people who have nowhere else to go but the street, its fun and free, want to go?"

"I'd love to."

It turned out to be the best time I've had in a very long time everybody was dancing, even me, the klutz. I swear I got kissed a hundred times at midnight, more friendly people I have seldom encountered in my life. We got back to the hotel about 3:00 a.m. I offered him a room at the hotel for the night but he declined,

"My dorm is only a 5-minute walk from here; I'll see you for brunch tomorrow." With that said he gave me an awkward hug and said, "You're an okay guy Carl, I'm glad you didn't freak out on me."

I slept soundly until 10:00, when the desk rang me on the hotel phone informing me I had a call, it was Nana, and very early in New York. She had spent the night with our foster kids, (I'll tell you about that later) after taking them, the older ones anyway, to the fireworks display.

She said she missed me, so did the kids and they sent their love, she had me crying on the phone because she was crying. She told me the NY time and we figured out the best time for both to call, at least twice a week.

No sooner had I hung up the room phone, my cell-phone rang, and Alexi informed me he was ready to eat.

"How long before you're ready to face the New Year? I'll be there in 15-minutes." The call ended. I added spontaneity to his list of positives, there were no negatives yet.

The days went by at lightning speed; the 2-week trial period came and went without comment by Alexi. I got the impression he let that go New Year's Eve because he never mentioned it again.

Chapter 2

Partners and brothers

About the middle of January we got a check for $2,500 for our first article, submitted just after New Years. Alexi's eyes bugged out and he exclaimed,

"I'm giving up engineering and becoming a writer, damn I never thought writing paid that well."

I got a brilliant idea; I sat Alexi down, "What do you think about us becoming partners?" I asked, "You've worked just as hard as I have, and the subject of the article was your idea, so you deserve an equal share of the profits. How about it partner?"

He put up a feeble argument that my boss wouldn't agree with it, and it was my job so I should get the bonuses, but he gave in, and settled on a 50-50 split. We agreed not to spend our windfall, seeing as everything else was paid for, including his daily $150. We would leave it in the bank in a joint account and be surprised at the end of the year.

With this agreement I knew I had won his trust, and I hope his respect. I certainly trusted and respected him, he was tenacious and tireless whenever we started a new project, and seemed to anticipate problems before they became harmful to the outcome.

By the end of March we had sent in eleven articles, and although they didn't all bring us a $2,500 commission check, they were still fat and juicy, we were like a smooth running machine.

Alexi was a born diplomat with what the Irish call the 'gift of gab'; I don't think we ever had one person he approached refuse to answer his questions. Our personal relationship was in good shape too, I asked him if he trusted me enough to go on the road together, he shocked the hell out of me by answering,

"Carl, I'm not afraid of you hitting on me, you could have any guy you set your mind to get. I see the way guys look at you, and you don't even seem to notice, I admit I was dead wrong about gays, and you in particular, you're the most honorable person our age that I have ever met, and I don't say *that* lightly."

That was the day I was sure I was in love with him, and in a truckload of trouble. For days I was a mass of jangling nerves, but gradually I learned again the secret of hiding my feelings as I had done with my father when I was six. Then it was because of hate, now it was love, and if Alexi knew, it would be the end of our story.

Unrequited love sounds like a disease, it's as painful and anxiety ridden. At night I would lie awake and wonder what Alexi was doing, was he out on a date? Was he home in bed with a lover? I decided to tell him, and end the charade. I kept putting it off, trying to screw up my courage just to lose him; it didn't seem fair.

In early April, Alexi asked me if I would go to his parents' home in Brno, it was their thirtieth wedding anniversary, and he had to go,

"You have to come too, they invited you, and I told them you would come."

He didn't intend to accept a refusal. You're already up to you knees in trouble Carl, might as well make it up to the hips; the outcome will be the same however deep you're in.

Reluctantly I agreed to meet his parents, not something I looked forward to. If I told Alexi the truth he would tell his parents, and they would hate me for trying to corrupt their only child. The last chance fruit of their loins, his mother was almost forty when she conceived Alexi, his father almost fifty. He was their miracle baby, and that's the truth; he's a miracle by any yardstick.

I wasn't ready for the surprise when we pulled up the long drive to his parent's house; it was a sixteenth or seventeenth-century building completely renovated. Floor-to-ceiling windows and the slate roof had been replaced.

The chimneys had new stylish spark arrestors that fit the architecture, which I couldn't identify except that it was old. It had new copper gutters and downspouts that fit as if they were original, I don't think they bothered with rain gutters back then.

The house had massive stone walls at least 2-feet thick, judging from the setback of the huge carved oak entry door. The walls rose 30-feet up to a crenulated parapet the width of the structure, about 60-feet, and set forward about 10-feet from the gable end of a very steep pitched roof with four large dormers on each side.

Above the entry was a single-story, 30-foot wide Porte cochere where the circular drive passed beneath. It too had a crenulated parapet held up by graceful arches. A frieze was carved into the stone running around the arches depicting hunting scenes, horses, and wild animals, amazingly, still discernible.

Alexi noted my surprise and gave me a 2-minute history lesson about the house. Built in the mid-seventeen-hundreds by a Romanian nobleman as a hunting lodge in what was then wilderness. The house was later abandoned, probably because of a change of royalty, and consequently, fell into disrepair.

When Alexi's parents found the old lodge it was little more than a ruin, the slate roof was stripped, windows torn out, and anything useful on the inside hauled away, the age-old practice of recycling.

The entry door was festooned with carvings of men on horseback with bows and arrows, hunting dogs, and wild boars. It had withstood the elements due to the Porte cochere and the recessed location in the wall, and survived because of its size and weight.

The door was a museum piece; beautifully carved and perfectly balanced, it moved with the pressure of one finger, it's hard to find that kind of workmanship today.

Alexi's parents bought the house while vacationing with friends who had a cabin in the mountains. On a horseback trip through the foothill area they came upon the dilapidated structure and were enthralled.

The ownership was investigated and found it had reverted to the government; their friends assured them the government, chronically short of funds, would be happy to get rid of what amounted to, in the government's estimation, a pile of debris.

For the ridiculously low price of 200,000-crowns, approximately $10,000, the property was purchased. It included; 5-acres of land, a deeded access to the main road, and a stream running through the property. Shortly thereafter his mother became pregnant, and they began to envision a new life in the country.

The house was not isolated in the wilderness, just setback from the road where it was hidden, there were houses, schools, churches, and shops, only 1000-feet down the road, but they seemed miles away.

Still living in Prague, they began the Herculean task of rebuilding the ancient structure. Five-years later, when Alexi was almost four, they relocated to Brno. The house was fully renovated, and the only stricture placed on the renovation work was that they couldn't alter the historic footprint of the building. This was the only home Alexi had ever known, and he was clearly at home here.

My moment of truth arrived by the massive door opening, and a very elegant lady stepping out to meet us, she embraced her son, and quickly turned to me,

"You must be Carl, I've heard only good things about you, I'm Barbra Duburk, welcome to our home."

"And a beautiful home it is." I answered, "Thank you for inviting me to share your family's celebration; I haven't had one before this."

"You'll have to tell me about that, we'll make this a special event just for you to remember. Now come inside and meet Lexi's father, he was on a phone call from the university when you drove up, he's probably finished by now."

Still feeling the trepidation, I let Alexi take hold of my arm and gently steer me into the house, He didn't realize the calming effect his hand on my arm had. There in the cavernous entry hall stood a handsome distinguished man in his sixties I reckoned, slim and fit still, he was an older version of Alexi. I extended my hand, and he completely ignored it, instead, he put his arms around me and kissed my cheek.

"We've asked Lexi to invite you up here a few times now; Barbra and I planned a trip to Prague to meet you if he didn't bring you along. He's been telling us about you since New Years, and the suspense has become unbearable, so his mother gave him a direct order; bring you or face the consequences."

"I can see where Alexi gets his kindness, I never expected a reception like this," I managed to get out without my voice cracking, but I couldn't stop my eyes from tearing up, "Thank you for having me Mr. Duburk."

"It's Ivan or Dad, no Mr. Duburk; I'd be honored if you would call me Dad but if you're uncomfortable with that, then its Ivan."

"Calling you by your first name seems disrespectful so I guess it'll be Dad." I could barely keep myself from blubbering, but always the white knight to the rescue, Alexi came and put his arm around my shoulders and said,

"I guess we're brothers now Carl, welcome to the family." A flood of emotion was raging through my body; happiness, gratitude, confusion, and mostly love.

"And what a handsome pair of brothers they are," his mother quipped, "I can imagine you two turning many heads in Prague, but in Brno you may be mobbed thinking you're Hollywood stars shooting a movie here, be careful."

The mother's teasing musical voice and her son's comforting touch dispelled all my forebodings, after days of worry and fretting over how things might be, I relaxed-what a relief.

"Mother has lunch ready for us so let's eat and hear what you two are up to." Dad said as he shepherded us into a kitchen straight out of Architectural Digest. The rear wall of the kitchen was floor-to-ceiling glass. The stone wall had fallen down and rather than rebuild it with stone, they installed a wall of glass facing east.

The kitchen was flooded with bright sunlight. In front of the glass was a large, round table with 6-chairs in the medieval style, you could easily accommodate twelve at that table.

Hanging over the table was a 5-foot diameter, antique, wrought-iron chandelier, with 8-fat candles each sitting in a saucer shaped holder. The visual effect of the very old and the very new was a stroke of genius by someone.

"Who designed the rehab?" I asked.

"Mom did, wait until you see the rest of the house," Alexi proudly spoke up, "She's a fantastic designer, but loves medicine better."

Mom rolled her eyes as if to say that's bullshit. "The place had to be gutted, modern facilities installed, every room electrified, and insulated, central heat, and A/C installed, all without making them noticeable or at least minimally noticeable."

"After the place was gutted and cleaned up you could see the potential of the space, Dad and I spent most of the year designing and redesigning until we had it the way we wanted it. Meanwhile, the roof was rebuilt, a septic system installed, electric lines brought in underground from the road, and crumbling walls repaired and shored up."

"When it was time to start the interior, I made it a point to be on the property as much and as often as I could. I had taken maternity leave, so my little angelface and I became general contractors."

"Twenty-years ago Czech men were more chauvinistic than now; in their eyes a woman knew nothing about building. It took a long time to get them to realize they had to do it the way I wanted it. Enough about that we want to know about you two, and your plans."

I thought that was my cue so I began. "I'm sure Alexi has told you what we're doing, but the main mission is the vampire rumor, you've heard about that, right?" their heads bobbed in unison so I continued, "Alexi thought you may have some influence with the medical examiner or whoever does autopsies in Prague."

"Could you possibly get copies or at least read them yourself, then tell us if there's a chance that all the blood had been drained from these two people?"

"My understanding of exsanguination is limited, but for a person to bleed to death the heart has to beating, right?" their heads nodded again, "And if the body dies before bleeding to death the blood collects at the lowest point of the corpse."

"That's right, but other factors could account for the loss of the blood, for instance; the location of the wound, or wounds, combined with the position the corpse was left in." Dr. Mom added, clarifying my theory.

"Let's assume they were attacked by wolves or bears after suffering hypothermia, multiple tearing bites would account for a large blood loss because in hypothermia the blood migrates to the center of the body to keep the vital organs warm."

"The attacking animals would also go for the warm center of the torso, which would quickly drain off the blood; if the body is in an inclined position with the wounds at the low point, the body could lose 90% of its blood. It's unusual for one body, but highly suspicious to find two bodies completely drained of their blood."

"Then there may be more to this than the official report?"

"We don't know if the bodies were drained completely, what we hear is that a local claims to have heard an EMT make a statement that it appeared no blood was left in the bodies. The other EMT asked him how he made that observation, and he said,"

"Because there are no signs of lividity on either body,"

"That doesn't mean, necessarily that they were drained of their blood and dumped in the forest." Mom concluded.

"Do you think an autopsy could show the cause of death considering the condition of the bodies?" I asked, getting into the investigating reporter persona.

"They could get to a point where an educated guess would determine natural causes or a slaying."

"So do you have any connections in the Medical Examiner's office?"

She thought for a minute and said, "I know people who will tell me what the MEs conclusions were, but as I understand it, the government is keeping everything very hush-hush. If they thought they had a leak, there would be hell to pay."

"I don't want trouble from the authorities that information would be used to determine what path we would head down to get to some semblance of truth."

"I appreciate that Carl; I'll make a couple of phone calls from the hospital, no trace that way."

"My partner and I thank you, right Alexi?"

A strange look passed from Mom to Alexi and from Dad to Alexi, "I didn't tell them about that I wanted to surprise them in December," he said, "Around here I'm called just Lexi, Carl, no A needed. Mom, Dad, Carl asked me to be his partner and share the commissions 50-50."

"Carl has a belief that I am as responsible for our success as he is, and that if I do half the work I should get half the commission. He's a little crazy I think, but maybe I am too because I agreed and now we're partners, very successful partners I might add."

"Don't denigrate or minimize your role in this," I said, jumping back in, "Without you I'd still be standing outside the Majestic Hotel looking for a translator." I turned to his parents and said, "Your son is unique, I'm sure you know that, but how many strangers have told you that?"

"He's a brilliant guy, working together we've gone way farther than I could have alone. He deserves half the rewards, and that's what he's going to get," turning back to Lexi I apologized, "I'm sorry I ruined your surprise, you should have told me it was a secret."

"There's no problem Carl, they understand I like to spring surprises on them, only good ones, and this one is really good."

Dad spoke up, "We're surprise early, but still surprised, it's heartening to hear someone say good things about you, I guess we did something right in raising you. Now let's end this lunch. Lexi would you help your mother clean up, I want a word with Carl."

He led me to a large library that still had a cozy feel to it, more of Mom's design genius no doubt. We sat facing each other in comfortable leather chairs in front of an ornate sandstone fireplace. I was curious about this private chat, but there was no indication of hostility or scorn. He put me at ease immediately by saying,

"Lexi understands the psychiatrist part of me that wants to know how people's minds work. I took this opportunity to get acquainted with you, and give Barbara the chance to grill Lexi about you. Barbara told me you said something to the effect of never having experienced a family celebration, are you an orphan?"

"No," I replied, "My father is very much alive I don't know whether my mother is alive or dead, she disappeared when I was six. She was a very unhappy lady she cried almost constantly, except when we could be together. My father thought she was coddling me, and turning me into a faggot, his word, not mine."

"Did he say this in your presence?"

"In my presence?" I laughed, "He called me that to my face since I was three."

"I can't believe a father would treat his son that way," Lexi's father was incredulous, "Was he your biological father?"

"Oh, yes, I'm sure he had all the tests done, if I weren't his son, I'd have been on the street in a heartbeat."

"I hate to be blunt, but is your father insane?"

"No, he's just extremely cold and cruel."

"How did you become such an exemplary young man living with a negative role model?"

"By staying out of his way, minding my Ps and Qs, and becoming invisible."

"Was he physically abusive to you or your mother?"

"Not to me, although he would raise his arm as if to strike me, then just walk away, I never saw him strike my mother, but he made her cry at every encounter."

"Did he continue to call you faggot after your mother left?"

"That was the only way he ever addressed me unless there was someone else present, then he wouldn't even address me."

"What were your feelings toward your father?"

"I hated him, loathed him, despised him, and wished him dead twenty times a day until I was eleven, then he sent me away to school."

"You stopped hating him?"

"Hardly, he was just out of my everyday life and I didn't dwell on him so much."

"He left you alone at school?"

"No way, a control freak doesn't give up that easily."

"How did you do at the private school?"

"Great, I was way ahead of the other kids, but I never had other kids around, so I had a hard time dealing with their pranks and jokes. I was very naïve and gullible."

"How long did you stay at the school?"

"Until my father yanked me out when I was 2-months from my thirteenth birthday."

"Why did he yank you out of school?"

"The headmaster called him and told him I wasn't accessing the expense account provided by my father, and when they searched my room they found 200-dollars in my dresser. I knew nothing about this until he arrived at the school like a thunderstorm, screaming at me for answers when I didn't even know what he was asking."

"The headmaster asked me where I got the 200-dollars. I was amazed they could be making such a fuss about this small sum of money, so I explained that I was paid by other students for violin lessons, tutoring in math, algebra, and English. They demanded names, which I gave them, and they called each in to refute my story. Each boy sheepishly admitted he had paid me for helping him with his studies."

"That enraged my father even more, I think than if I had stolen the money, he screamed."

"I didn't send you here to be lowly goddamn teacher, I provide you with a large amount of money, why are you debasing yourself by stooping to this level for money?"

"The headmaster was dumbstruck; I was so embarrassed I had to fight back so I screamed just as loudly, 'Because I don't want your fucking money'. This time he did hit me, he punched me on the side of my head, and by the time my head stopped spinning we were in the limo heading home."

"I'm getting the impression that your father is wealthy, is that the case?"

"A filthy rich man, yes," I said bitterly, "Emphasis on filthy."

"Where did you go to school before the boarding school?"

"I've had private tutors as long as I can remember; Nana was the only person beside my mother, the tutors, and my music teachers with whom I had contact."

"What did you study with the music teachers?"

"Violin and piano."

"Can you play either?"

"Both actually, but I stopped studying when I was thirteen."

"We have a grand piano in the great-room, will you play for us?"

"I haven't played for years; maybe when nothing's going on, I can practice a while."

"Why was thirteen the high-water mark?"

"When I was thirteen he threw me out of the house."

"I think you should just tell me the story your answers are boggling my mind."

"When we got back from the school, he kept telling me that I would regret what I did to him at the school. I knew reason wouldn't work on him so I said nothing, hoping he would go away. He didn't go away. He rehired the tutors and nana, and I was a prisoner again."

"A couple of months went by and my violin teacher suggested I send a demo recording to Juilliard to see if they would accept me, he said I had learned all he could teach me, and I needed a more advanced teacher."

"My father had a Stradivari, I had played it only twice before the private school fiasco, once when he was in an expansive mood, and once when my grandparents were visiting. My teacher went to him and asked if I could play it to cut the demo, and miracles still happen, he agreed."

"I was thrilled, the violin sang for me, it took me away from Earth to, I don't know where, and I didn't care. I was not only naïve and gullible, I was also stupid. So the unsuspecting dupe cut the demo playing the Stradivari and mailed it off to Juilliard with a letter from my teacher who claimed the demo was my best yet."

"Two-weeks to thirteen, the police rang at our front door, the butler let them in. We were told my grandparents had been killed in a plane crash with my father's brother, his wife, and 2-sons ages six and eight, his sister, and her husband, the pilot, and copilot, my grandfather's secretary, and two cabin attendants.

"My maternal grandmother had died when I was a baby and Papa died 2-years after my mother left. Now I had no family except him. At the funeral I was approached by a short fat man with a funny hat, a bowler, I think it's called. He introduced himself as Matt Sherman, my grandparent's lawyer."

"He took me aside and explained that some time before their death my grandparents had changed the deeds on several pieces of property. Their Fifth Avenue town-house was one, also the plane that crashed was in my name, the plane, only 1-year-old, was insured for the replacement cost of 50-million-dollars. All the property and insurance money would be held in trust, but the house could be lived in at any time.

"A maintenance fund was already set up for 5-year intervals that took care of the staff; a housekeeper, cook, two maids, a gardener, and the chauffer. It also included the utilities, taxes, insurance, two vehicles, and any repairs for the house, and cars. It didn't register in my grieving brain then, so he gave me his card and told me to call him anytime if I needed him."

"I went home with Nana, and a week later found a letter in my room from Juilliard. I was shaking nervously as I opened it and started reading the letter from the director of Juilliard. To sum up what he said was that I had no technical expertise, and it appeared as if the demo had been enhanced in a studio."

"I hadn't cried for a long time before this, but I did then, for hours. At some time during my crying jag I shoved the letter back in the envelope, and I noticed another page in there, my father had written a note after opening my letter, it said, 'too bad faggot, you play the piano as if someone is banging on the keys with a hammer, and Juilliard said it all about your violin playing. Maybe you could get a job with Hoe Down as a fiddler, that's more your style'."

"I had never felt such rejection, shame, and bitterness all together, before this or after, I promised myself then, I would never play the violin again. Since then I haven't picked up a violin, it's been 13-years, but I still feel the Stradivari singing for me."

"Words can't describe the hate I felt for him, it ate at me constantly for weeks. Then I woke up, hating him was hurting me more than it was hurting him. I realized it was having no effect at all on him; he was reveling in the destruction and pain he had caused."

"The very next day I called Matt Sherman, and asked him to notify the staff of my grandparent's home to prepare the house for four more occupants. I knew it would be impossible to live in the same house as that monster, and keep my sanity."

"I deliberately started an argument, knowing exactly how it would end. I convinced Nana that she should witness the fireworks, and I was armed with a recorder, wired, as they call it. I accused him of setting up the whole Juilliard fiasco,"

"How can you be such a miserable bastard to your only son?" I asked him.

"You have some respect," he replied, "I'm your father."

"That was the response I was waiting for, and I screamed back at him what I had rehearsed the previous night, 'You are NOT my father, you have NEVER been my father, you were only a sperm donor.' It worked, he lost his temper."

"Get out of my house, you fucking little faggot. I can't stand to look at you or hear your whining, you are no longer my son and heir."

"Nana was standing there with her jaw hanging open, she was always skeptical when I told her what he called me, there's no better proof than hearing it firsthand, and she was in the 'Am I hearing what I'm hearing?' mode."

"We packed up our belongings, and retrieved my journals, 10-year's worth from the secret cabinet my mother had Papa build for me. I also took some keepsakes, and a few of my mother's things that I had managed to salvage after my vengeful sperm donor went on his destructive rampage."

"Mr. Sherman had instructed the chauffer to pick me up; when he arrived we were waiting at the front door with our pitiful pile of bags, looking like refugees from a disaster. That was the day my life really began."

"We'll talk some later Carl," he said in a kindly manner "Lexi must be wondering if I've got you under hot lights. You gave me a lot to digest, and I appreciate your openness." I think there were tears in his eyes.

CHAPTER 3

LEXI'S HOME AND PARENTS

Lexi and his mother were indeed waiting for us in the 'great-hall' as it was originally called, with 15-foot high ceilings. You would think the cavernous room would make you feel as if you were in a public building, such as a public library or city hall.

With the intricate dark stained coffered ceilings, a massive truss of the same colored wood every 12-feet and chandeliers that looked original, one between each truss, made the room's ceiling seem closer and less dwarfing than if it were a regular ceiling.

The fireplace was original; 6-people walking abreast could step into it without ducking their heads. It would take a couple of good size trees to fill that fire pit. To heat the room on its own, it probably needed that many every couple of hours.

A magnificent black lacquered grand piano dominated the great room along with contemporary furniture of the era, though how much searching to find these treasures compelled me to ask,

"Where did you find all this furniture? I know they're not reproductions but they look almost new."

"They're not reproductions," Mom answered, "Eastern Europe is awash with antiques, our dealer in Brno knows every old estate in a 1,000-kilometer-radius including; Poland, Germany, Austria, Slovakia, and especially Vienna. Much of it in this room came from the Vienna area, he had each piece restored, refinished, and reupholstered."

"After seeing this room he recommended the brocade for all the upholstered pieces, and the drapes for the windows at either end of the room. I was concerned that the effect might be too dark and depressing; however, that didn't happen, it worked the way he envisioned it."

The room didn't necessarily look like a hunting lodge; it was more like the pictures I'd seen of the multimillion-dollar chalets in the California and Colorado mountains, in a word—stunning.

We sat and chatted for a while then Lexi made a suggestion, "Why don't I show you the rest of the house and yard?"

"I'm up for that," I answered, "But I'm not sure I can take it in all at once, it's astonishingly beautiful, like stepping backward in history"

"Flattery," Mom quipped, "Will get you everywhere. Go familiarize yourself with the house, and we'll see you in an hour or so."

On the opposite side of the entry hall was a pair of pocket doors with stained glass panels set into the top half of the doors. The stained glass depicted cornucopias, fruits and vegetables spilling from wicker horns.

Open doors revealed a dining-room with wainscoting easily 8-foot-high, paneled in squares, a ledge at the top displayed glass and china serving pieces interspersed with beer steins of pewter and china.

A 16-foot long, heavy, old table with huge intricately carved legs held sway in this room. Around the table sat 12-chairs in the same style, and four more at intervals around the room.

At the end of the room toward the kitchen was a built-in-buffet with a glass-door-hutch above it. On the wall between the buffet top and the hutch, the paneling retracted into the wall behind the hutch to facilitate the serving of food.

Beside the buffet was a door leading into a butler's pantry with cabinetry on 3-sides done with the same, precise craftsmanship of all the woodwork I'd seen to this point.

On the floor of the pantry, two plank trap-doors each 3-foot wide and 8-foot long were set flush with the stone tiles. An iron ring was recessed into the edge of each door close to the ends; Lexi gave me his little grin and asked me,

"Do you want to see the dungeon?"

I thought he was kidding, but he lifted the very heavy doors with no exertion whatever, I saw 2-cylinders at the other side of the opening, clearly hydraulic openers. Stone steps led down into complete darkness, he stepped down to the first step, and the lights came on.

Proceeding down the stairs I saw he wasn't kidding, some cell doors had pieces of rusted iron bars still present, but most doors were long gone, the survivors were left there for effect.

"We use this as a cold cellar now; the temperature is a constant 55 to 60-degrees, perfect for vegetables and some fruit." Lexi said.

The walls were most likely 10-foot thick to provide a stable footing for the stone walls above, making the dungeon an unexpected feature of the house. Through that pantry was another pantry, this one for storage of food supplies for the kitchen, but done in the same inimitable style.

An archway took us into the kitchen where we had eaten, and then into the entry again. Lexi led me up a wide, curved, stone staircase with a semicircular wall on one side reaching to the ceiling of the second-floor. A curved half-wall sat on the handrail side from the floor to about 3-feet above each step.

An expertly curved 12-inch-wide and 3-inch-thick, black-walnut plank sat atop the half-wall, carved to provide a handgrip, and finished to a shiny, almost black hue. This had to be new; there wasn't a nick or a scratch on the entire surface.

"It's original," Lexi said, proving me wrong, "someone tried to remove it at one point, but the rail has a spline fitted into the stone about 10-inches deep they literally built the rail into the stone, it must weigh at least 500-pounds."

"I'll show you at the top where a pry bar gouged it trying to lift it off the stone. It didn't move even 1-millimeter. Mom harassed the wood workers to sand it down so no nicks or scratches showed."

"They rebelled when she insisted they repair the gouges upstairs, and compromised with a small cap made of the same wood, fitted under the end of the rail where someone had tried to free it from the stone."

We had just reached the second-floor; he bent down and pulled a small block of wood from halfway under the rail, revealing deep grooves on the underside end of the rail. I had to agree with Mom, it couldn't stay like that, it was ugly, and the workers were right, it was irreparable.

The cap was an inspiration; it looked like a planned, finished end piece. A small point though was why didn't they put one at the bottom also? I didn't voice that thought.

The curved stairs emptied onto the side of a 10-foot wide hall with large double doors to the right. Three more doors on each side of the hall, and 3-doors at the end of the hall, the middle, wider one, led to the attic or attics.

From the size of the roof there could be two, or three more floors up there. On each side of the attic door was a narrower door, which had to be linen closets.

A 4-foot wide Oriental rug ran the entire length of the hall, fifty-feet at least. The width and the height of the doors were of necessity larger than the standard door, to keep them in perspective to the size of the hall. Similarly, the windows in the bedrooms looked normal-sized until you realized they were so big it would take 2-people to open them.

The double doors opened on the master suite, which ran the full width across the front of the house. Four French doors gave access to a large terrace on the roof of the porte cochere, 30-feet by 30-feet.

Small potted trees, flower boxes, a glass-topped wrought-iron table, and chairs, two chaise longue, and an exercise machine all sat on a handsome terrazzo marble floor. The floor was basic coffee brown with shards of green and gold, possibly glass, very nice effect.

Large arched openings in the middle of each sidewall created his and hers bathrooms, or en-suites as they're called in Europe. Through each arch was a vestibule with a large-arched top, stained-glass window, dressing rooms, on one side of each vestibule, and the bathrooms on the other, very classy.

Diagonally in one corner of the room was a gigantic canopy bed about half the size of a football field, at least 4-feet off the floor. A set of stairs with 3-steps sat on each side of the bed.

A fireplace faced the foot of the bed on the opposite wall, elegantly clad in white carrera marble with a matching hearth. Lexi told me it came from an old estate in Slovakia, wherever it came from it was gorgeous. Oriental rugs sat atop dark-oak plank-flooring that continued throughout the second-floor.

Lexi's bedroom was to the left of the stairs, large, with its own bath, and simply furnished, probably to the satisfaction of the teenage boy who lived in it.

Two more bedrooms opened off the hall. One office for both doctors was next, with an antique partner's desk sitting in the middle of the room. Beside the office was an activity room as they called it, a better name would be workshop, but it was like the rest of the house, well planned and nicely furnished.

A fully outfitted gymnasium was last in the line. It blew my mind, no wonder Lexi was so physically fit, and buff, he'd been working out all his life in this perfect place to grow up.

He led me to the room next to his that would be my room, it was nicely furnished with a four poster-bed, armoire, dresser, night stands, an easy chair with side table and a floor lamp for reading, the ubiquitous Oriental rug, and, of course, its own bath.

Being in the room next to Lexi was disconcerting at first, but as I thought about it I felt somehow we were coming closer together, if only he thought that way too.

The yard, as Lexi called it, was more like a park. Five acres is not a small lot, it's 220,000-square-feet, that's a huge area for a child to romp in, with tall mature trees to climb. A small stream ran through the yard that fed into, and back out of a sizable pool. The stream had been widened, and dredged out, then the bottom and sides covered with sand.

Fully grown oaks, chestnuts, and a few species of evergreens, shaded the pool. Ropes hung from the limbs of several trees, and I pictured Lexi and his friends cavorting in this perfect setting.

I never had enough knowledge to be envious of how other kids lived, but I was envious that day, I wanted so badly to be a kid again and be here with my brother Lexi, but as the saying goes, 'Wishing and a buck gets you on the bus.'

Saturday was the anniversary celebration, catered by a 5-star restaurant in Brno. The house bustled with activity all day. With nothing to do that would be useful, I went to the great room and ran some scales on the recently tuned piano, the tone was perfect.

After a little thought, I decided to play Franz Liszt's Hungarian Rhapsody number six after dinner, that would liven up any party.

Playing a few bars to see if I could do it without looking like a fool, I got into the piece and was going strong. It came back to me as if I had never stopped playing; I was going to be okay. I finished the piece, and behind me clapping started, I turned to see Lexi looking at me with wonder,

"You're just full of surprises, I would never have thought that you could play like that, were you a concert pianist?"

"Unlikely, my father would never have allowed that."

"Why not? You're good; hell you're better than good you were excellent. You could be famous and rich; wouldn't he want that for you?"

"He wouldn't care. I'll tell you about my father one day when my stomach is strong enough to talk about him."

"I can't wait to hear this; it sounds like a family feud. Dad said you were going to play for us, is tonight the night?"

"I think it would be a real opportunity to do something useful for this celebration. What do you think of this plan? After dinner, you announce that coffee and cordials will be served in the great-room. When the guests are in the room, you ask me to play something on the piano."

"You will already have instructed the caterers to wheel the anniversary cake into the great-room to be served there. When I finish the piece you dim the lights as a signal that the caterers wheel in the cake, and I'll start playing the wedding march."

"It's great Carl, Mom and Dad will love it."

Waiting for the guests to arrive, appetizers were served; pate, petite quiche, cheese puffs, a Czech pastry filled with a delicious meat concoction, and a dozen others, but the pastry was my favorite. The guests arrived slowly, and by 7:00 we were seated for dinner.

The menu started with a cauliflower and artichoke soup, followed by a coquille St. Jacques–tiny scallops in a cream sauce, next, an endive salad. The main course was Beouf en croute with a Bordelaise sauce, in America its beef wellington with gravy.

The main course was complimented with a mixture of baby carrots, pearl onions, small red potatoes, and broccoli florets. Vintage '97, Chateau Haut-Brion French Bordeaux wine was served throughout the meal, excellent wine and a superb choice.

The meal was a resounding success. Lexi made our announcement, not what Mom had planned, but thought Lexi had an idea to relieve our sated condition.

When coffee and after dinner drinks were served, Lexi was with the plan, and I played the Hungarian Rhapsody for them. Immediately at the last note the lights dimmed, Lexi opened the doors for the caterer, and I started the Wedding March, all at the same instant as if we had rehearsed it.

Mom had tears running down her cheeks and Dad was choked too, Lexi was beaming with happiness. Mom was taken completely by surprise, Dad not so much because he had asked me to play for them, but didn't know it would be tonight, and for their guests also.

Mom said she was going to adopt me and Dad agreed. Effusive thanks and praise went on for an hour; I felt a little self-conscious intruding on their anniversary, what should have been their night. When I told Lexi on the trip home, he said I was paranoid; Mom and Dad were thrilled by what we did.

By Monday, we were acting like we'd been family forever, the house was so full of love you had to relax and it wrapped around you. I felt like part of a family for the first time. Dad caught up to me as I was on my way to the back patio,

"Lexi and Mom are going into Brno to the hospital so Mom can make some phone calls to get the information you asked for," he said, "I thought we could continue our talk if you're up for it."

"I am, I haven't told a soul about my childhood or my family, talking to you on Friday was cathartic, I'm no longer reticent about my past."

"Let's talk out here it's a beautiful day." He suggested, "I want to ask you about something you said on Friday. When you left your father's house you said you took 10-years of journals with you, were you writing in a journal at three?"

"That's when my mother started me on it, yes, it was very childish at first, written in crayon with atrocious spelling, but she let me go at my speed, and with my words, which she suggested. I was learning, but my writing didn't improve until I was six. When she left I pored my frustration and loneliness into my journals. I was writing quite well by then, and not with crayons."

"She had her father, build me a secret cabinet in my closet so my father couldn't find them, if he had, he would for sure have destroyed them. He never knew I kept a journal, even when he took all my belongings from school he didn't check my laptop.

I transferred them to my pc and printed them whenever I went home. I still keep a daily log of events and finances, but the emotional aspect is ammunition for prying eyes, so I don't write about them."

"I would like to read those early 10-years of journals if you would let me."

"No problem, I'll call Nana and get her to airship them to you here within a few days. I tried to read them, but the whole bad scene came back to me after reading only a few days of that time, I couldn't go on."

"Thank you Carl, I think the journals will give me some insight into your early life and maybe relieve your anxiety. This is privileged information; it's between us, Lexi and Barbara won't know of our talks if you don't want them to know. There's one other thing I have to ask you, *are* you gay?"

"Yes," I replied with no hesitation, "I am."

"I'm convinced your father sensed that in you at a very early age, it's not uncommon, but a wait and see attitude is usually the accepted way to go. Your father must have some serious issues with homosexuality to be so aggressive toward you."

"Homosexuality was never discussed; when I started to read I checked in the dictionary for the word faggot, and found a faggot is a homosexual man. Even reading the definition of homosexual didn't give me any understanding of why he called me that, I wasn't a man."

"One more thing and you don't have to answer. Do you love Lexi?"

"Yes, so much it hurts."

"I thought so, well stop hurting, he loves you too." My stunned silence prompted him to continue, "I know my son. First, you are the only person he has ever brought home, no frat brothers, no girls—never even discussed them with me or his mother."

"Second, you may not realize it, but his eyes shine when he looks at you, when you two talk he gets a goofy grin on his face. When he talks to us about you, he has nothing but praise and respect for you, before I met you I thought you could walk on water. Now I know why he feels like that and I'm sure he'll come to realize what is going on. He says he's not seeing anyone so what can you deduce from all this?"

"You just removed a whole lot of anxiety from my life," I said, "Before coming here I agonized that you and Mom would hate me if you knew I were gay, that you would think I was trying to corrupt your only son and that would be the end of my imaginary love affair with Lexi. Whether he's in love with me or not, I feel a lot more comfortable about him, and you and Mom."

"That's a natural reaction to an unknown situation Carl, Barbara and I would be thrilled if you and Lexi got together. Barbara asked me last night whether you were the one who would open his closet door, I replied that I hope so and she said she did too."

I thought I was going to cry, I tried to change the conversation so I wouldn't, "Lexi will be finished at the University in a couple of weeks, so he won't have the dorm anymore. I've had it with hotel living and have been looking for an apartment, do you think I should ask Lexi to share an apartment with me?"

"Yes I do, I'll wager that he will accept. Don't promise him anything, no conditions, just 50-50 on cleaning, cooking, and shopping. Ask him tonight after dinner, we'll leave you alone for a while and you can talk in private, look for the signs I told you about. Now, let's go make some dinner for our detectives."

When Lexi and Mom got home, they were like schoolgirls eager to pass on a secret. We served them dinner, and sat at the kitchen table, Mom started,

"It seems there may be something the government doesn't want us to know. A Doctor I work with quite often has a daughter who works in the coroner's office, she told him about the autopsy, and how secretive the ME's Office was. The autopsy did state there was no blood left in either body, one body is coincidence, two, is suspicious."

"The bodies showed evidence of sexual assault, but due to the deterioration of the flesh the determination was uncertain. A fluid found on both bodies remains unidentified, but it wasn't from an animal or human, the mutilation of the bodies was caused by animals according to bite marks, and tearing patterns."

"The staff was warned not talk about it as it was not for public consumption. They probably have no more clues than we do; you boys feel it has to be investigated, am I right?"

Lexi chimed in with "You want to believe it, right Carl?" I wanted to jump up and kiss him, he was so eager, and innocent, and so damned beautiful. I glanced over at Dad to find him with a knowing grin on his face that said 'I told you so.'

"Right Lexi, We have to be careful though, we don't want to cause any trouble for Mom, by getting the Doctor's daughter involved in an investigation looking for the leak. And we don't need to get into a pissing match with any bureaucrats, they always win, we might even be banned from that area, then, no story." I explained gently so I wouldn't lower his enthusiasm.

I needn't have worried, he was still as pumped as when they came home, eager to jump into this mess feet first. My God I love this boy. How am I going to hold it together until he gets his head on straight?

I just had to believe that he was worth every day of agony, and rely on Dad's prediction that he would find himself, and admit his true nature to his consciousness. His Psychiatrist, Dad, claimed his subconscious already knew the truth. I pledged to wait as long as it took and just to be near him was soothing my impatience.

While I was ruminating Lexi, was expounding on a way we could operate covertly,

"By making the locals believe we're going to increase tourist activity, we'll get them talking about what has happened since the bodies were discovered, and write about local color instead of the investigation."

He's smart too I added to myself, while Mom and Dad watched my open and naked admiration of their son.

"You just proved again why I wanted you to be my partner," I said and to the parents, "Has he got a knack for this stuff or what?"

They were beaming at the two of us as if their prayers had been answered, and their wishes granted, they were clearly pleased, and proud by what they were hearing.

"You compliment each other like milk and cookies, or peanut butter and jam." Mom said.

"Heckle and Jeckle," Lexi laughed, we all joined in.

"Seriously, guys," Dad opined, "You still have to tread very carefully, the 'bureaucrats' as you call them are suspicious to the point of paranoia, and will without your knowledge, be monitoring your every move, and intercepting every e-mail you send to NY. I have confidence in you that you'll make them conclude you know less than they do; they won't be satisfied until then."

"We'll develop a way of asking questions that won't raise suspicion or the government's hackles," Lexi replied, "Carl thinks I'm a diplomat in training, so I'll hone those skills, and make him proud of me."

My face was burning and I knew I was red, Dad didn't help by adding, "I think Carl is proud of you already son." I burned even hotter, "I think we're embarrassing him, let's take a break."

He turned toward me and winked. My God what a family, I don't think they have one secret held among the three of them, they're frank and guileless, I love them more every day.

"Come outside with me," I asked Lexi, "We can stretch our legs; I want to run something by you." He held the door open, and we stepped out into the slightly chilly, early April night.

"You're about to be without a room when this semester ends, how about you and I rent a two bedroom apartment, our expense account will cover the rent and utilities because it'll be cheaper than living at the hotel. We can share the chores like cooking and cleaning, and have a place to come home to when we finish a road trip. What do you think?"

Instead of answering me he pulled me into a long tight hug, I could feel and smell his sweet, hot breath on the side of my face and neck, my knees became rubbery, I thought I'd faint.

"You are the most awesome friend I've ever had," he whispered in my ear, "I've been hoping you'd ask me for days now. How could I refuse that? It's a solution for both of us, yes, yes, yes." Dad was right again, I guess he did know his son.

We walked for a while and spoke about what we would need to start a household. His parents had taught him well, he was no pampered, spoiled child, he had learned to prepare food, clean the kitchen, and knew what equipment we would need. Of necessity I was well versed in taking care of myself, so another fit was added to our friendship.

Back in the house again, Lexi broke the news, "We're gonna get an apartment together," he excitedly proclaimed. Dad gave me his 'I told you so' grin, "We're setting up a base of operations to save money and have a place to retreat to. I guess I won't be moving back home anytime soon."

Ever, if I can have my way, I thought.

Mom rejoined, "You make it sound like an espionage movie, I'm pleased that you'll be together, you can look after each other and not be alone."

I'm pleased too, Mom scores another win. At this rate they're going to do all my work winning Lexi over.

I must have looked like the cat that ate the canary because Dad inquired, "What do you think of it Carl, Will it work for you?"

Okay, enough embarrassment, "It's an ideal solution to several problems, we're very compatible and usually think alike, I don't see any major roadblocks, clear sailing all the way."

Lexi was grinning like an idiot and I became smiling idiot number two, soon Mom and Dad were grinning from ear to ear.

CHAPTER 4

MAY DAY IN THE MOUNTAINS

"Let's leave early tomorrow morning," Lexi suggested, "We have a lot to do, and I have to finish and turn in my Treatise by the twenty-first. I want to take the time to help you find a place for us to live; I can't wait for us to have our own place."

"The university area is a pretty good neighborhood, and according to other students, not all that expensive. You more or less know your way around there, and I wouldn't have to worry about you getting lost."

"Do you worry that I'll get lost?" I asked him.

"Yes I do," he quickly replied, "Sometimes at night when you say you're going out for a bite to eat, my stomach churns all night, and I want to call and check on you, but I don't want to be a mother hen. Living in the same place will put that to rest."

My brain was doing backflips; you lay awake, worrying about me? Welcome to the club, I lay awake thinking about you too. I wish you would wake up and see this for what it is, your father's right, you care a lot, maybe it's already love. Oh for the courage to say that to him, but I'll bide my time, and trust that Dad is right.

Back home, Lexi called and said he was almost finished with his treatise, so we could spend the day together looking for a place to live. He showed up at 7:00 a m with an arm load of magazines and newspapers ready to scour the want ads for the perfect apartment. Four-hours later we were no closer to housing than the day before.

Finally, I called my publisher; he recommended we buy a condo. In Prague condos are plentiful, apartments are scarce. Lexi was skeptical,

"How are we going to pay for a condo?" he asked in a panicky voice, "It'll take at least a $50,000-down payment. We don't have that kind of cash even with our commission account."

"With the publisher's money, of course," I said softly to calm him, "I mentioned that fact to him, and he volunteered to front the cost of buying the condo. We will own it, but when we sell it, the seed money goes back to him; any profit we make on the sale is ours. Do you think he has an ulterior motive by doing this?"

"I don't know, is he gay?"

"Got me," I shrugged, "He's 10-years older than God, so it's unlikely he would do it for that reason, but it may be to get us to do anything and everything for a prizewinning story."

"Meaning take risks we wouldn't normally take."

"Bingo, the magazine publishing business is pretty cutthroat, the journalists' creed is, 'anything for a story'. I'm not saying he wants us to do anything illegal, just walk real close to the line."

"Are you all right with that? I am if you are."

"Lexi, I intended to go all out for this gig, it could be a career maker or breaker, and the second part is unthinkable. If this works, I'll go freelance, then work anywhere in the world I want. Prague and New York would be my choice for a base. I don't know if your folks have adopted me, but I've adopted them, you guys are the family I never had, so it has to be Prague."

I could tell he was choked up; it took a couple of minutes for him to regain his control before starting to speak again,

"They feel the same way, so do I, I'm glad you want to live here, hell I'm on cloud nine, I thought that after this assignment you would leave and we'd lose touch."

"There's no way I could leave you, we're partners, and more."

"What's the 'more'?" he asked timidly as if he hoped the answer was the one he needed to hear.

"We met only 3-months ago, since then we've become partners, best friends, brothers, and now we're about to become roommates, raising the intimacy to a new level. The rapid transition from strangers to what we are now is amazing, and I wouldn't change one step of the journey even if I could. The final outcome will be what it will be; our attitudes toward each other will be the determining factor."

"That was right on point Carl, I agree 100%, I wouldn't change it in any way, either. At the speed we're evolving, by the end of the year we'll be acting like an old married couple."

I hoped that was a prescient statement, just leave out the old. I started wondering if gays could be married in the Czech Republic, I think I'll check that out. My fantasies were running wild, I'd seen many gay and lesbian couples in Prague walking hand-in-hand with no reaction from the local populace, I pictured Lexi and me walking that way in the park by the University; dream on about your sweet prince, stranger things have happened.

We found a condo a few blocks from the university in a quiet upscale neighborhood. Partially furnished, 2-master suites, gourmet kitchen, and downstairs, a fully equipped gym, Lexi loved it, his first home away from home. His first words as we looked around,

"Carl you choose which bedroom you want, you're the one who arranged all this, I'm going to make a list of what we need to fill the cupboards and refrigerator."

I can't seem to get him to accept the concept of equal partners. In every possible situation he wants me to have like now, first dibs of bedrooms, the lion's share of the commission, final say on job issues, and on and on. Partnership means, to me anyway, an equal division of work, and reward, period. If, or maybe I should say when, we finally get it together that's the way it has to be.

May Day celebrations were going on everywhere as we moved in. It gave us a euphoric feeling even if we were working. We didn't have that much to move so it really wasn't hard work, but the place needed organizing, and things put in their places. Lexi had celebrated May Day every year for his entire life, according to him very raucous and wild.

"Don't you want to be part of what's going on out there?" I asked him, "We can knock off for today if you want to join in the festivities."

"I would rather stay here with you so we can get this place set up like a real home, I don't want you to do all the work while I play. I really don't feel like playing I'm having a blast doing what we're doing right here."

There's progress here, he's maturing.

"I was thinking that if we get the condo ready to live in, we could take a couple of days to go up to the mountains, the roads are open and the weather forecast is warm and sunny for the next 5-days."

"That's a good idea Lexi, we could leave tomorrow morning," I said, "drive around up there Thursday and Friday, and then stop to see your parents for the weekend. We would be back in time for the graduation rehearsal, and have a little better idea of what hurdles we're facing."

"That's what I was thinking, we really are compatible aren't we?" he commented, "Great minds think alike."

We are way more compatible than either of us at this point could possibly dream, a connection is there, and we're seeing it clearer every day. Early the next morning we rented a midsize Yugo, and stopped at an electronic store to pick up a GPS device to prevent, as Lexi put it,

"Getting our heads messed with by the road system in the mountains, it's real easy to get turned around up there, and find out we're going backward. Let's have breakfast, and I'll call Mom to tell her to expect us Friday night."

Two-hundred-kilometers later we were entering Brno, an easy 2-hour ride on a 4-lane highway. Still only midmorning, we kept going another 55-kilometers to Hodonin where the main highway continued to Vienna or Slovakia, but the road to Hodonin branched off to the east. The going was considerably slower on the 2-lane road.

Hodonin, where we ate lunch, is a quaint little city of no more than 30,000-people, on the Morava River. It looked medieval in one place, then in an instant ultramodern glass and steel, high office buildings. The older buildings resembled Russian architecture somewhat like the Kremlin, the 'why' to that question, was unknown to Lexi.

Leading us into the Czech Carpathians was an ancient route winding through the foot-hills. It finally started climbing into the actual mountains about 30-kilometers from Hodonin as the crow flies, but for the winding around every obstacle the builders of the road encountered centuries ago.

It worsened the farther into the mountains we went, whoever marked the ultimate route of the road definitely took the path of least resistance, what should have been a 50-kilometer drive, was more like eighty or ninety.

The Czech area of the Carpathians was sparsely populated compared to the Polish, Slovakian, Ukrainian, and Romanian mountain areas. Probably because their roads were at least twentieth-century, these were more like from the Middle Ages.

No towns were listed by name on the map Lexi had brought with him, only small dots with numbers beside them. A product of the communist era, before that he opined, they probably didn't even have a number, just little hamlets known only to the locals, the only ones who cared.

Lexi had warned me of the drop-offs on these roads, I didn't take him seriously, just a little exaggeration. Nearly missing a turn, on my side of the road (what road?) was only empty space going down a mile, no rail, or barrier to prevent an impromptu flight, proved he wasn't exaggerating.

Midafternoon we came upon a village between the road and a swiftly flowing river. A sign in Czech posted just before the village that Lexi translated to read, 'highest road elevation in Czech Mountains, 2,100-meters–7,000-feet.

Across the river a scant half-kilometer, rose a ridge of peaks at least another 500-meters, still mantled in snow, and dazzlingly brilliant in the early May sunshine.

The view was breathtaking, the little village neat, clean, and very old. Every roof had the same shape, Lexi wondered why as I did. They started out as fairly steep pitch roofs, about two-thirds of the way to the peak, every roof took a jog upward, which about doubled the pitch. It would have been unique on one house, but here every house, barn, shed, and stable boasted the same eye-catching feature.

The little hamlet boasted a river walk with a few shops, a constable's office, a one-floor inn more like a motel, with doors facing the river. Three-hundred or 400-feet down from the inn was a little park with what looked like a band shell, although a very small one.

After the last hair-raising half-hour in the car, I desperately wanted to plant my feet on solid ground so we stopped to check the place out. The area widened out past the inn and shops, and there were several small farms visible, all with the same style roofs.

The great-room of the inn was at the far end of the building from the band shell where we had parked. We walked along the river walk to the Inn entrance, and the smell of cooking made our mouths water.

Several people were sitting at the bar, some in front of the fireplace warming up from the chilly, late-afternoon, mountain air. The people were friendly, as we walked across the room they smiled, or nodded greetings.

The Innkeeper was a middle-aged man, balding, and spreading in his girth, he had, however; an affable smile and a friendly greeting.

May Day celebrations here would last through the weekend, every night for 5-days they would drink, eat, dance, and sing. Tonight a whole roast pig cooking under the inn in a pit would be a feast for the village. The roast was what we smelled getting out of the car. He invited us to join the festivities, and said he had one room left if we wanted to stay.

Driving after dark there isn't recommended, especially after downing a few beers. Considering our incident during daylight hours, Lexi didn't have to repeat it after he translated for me.

When the bars patrons discovered I was an American, it became a love fest, everyone crowded around us asking Lexi questions. Every stereotype of perceived American lifestyle was explored; was I rich? Did I live in Hollywood? What kind of sports car did I drive? Are we going to open a Mc Donald's in the Carpathians? They wanted to shake my hand.

The furor finally died down, though they still were sitting in a circle around us. Lexi had them eating out of his hand, they were hanging on his every word. Now and then, he would inform me what he was telling them, but I'm sure he was embellishing just a little.

"The Czech government is paying Karel a fortune to write about the mountains, and the people, to bring much-needed Czech crowns to you people with economic problems."

He was feeding the five-thousand, they idolized him. I nudged him and said,

"You know, Lexi, we have to live up to your promises now or it won't be the castle they attack with pitchforks, it'll be us."

"I've already thought of that," he came back, "Account for the current rumors, by writing several true stories giving a hint of danger and intrigue. Then teach the locals how to make it work for them by marketing local art and handmade objets d'art, handmade embroidery, carvings, and a hundred other things."

"Show them how to do a flea market type operation, make food that tourists will suck-up such as Czech hamburgers and Czech hot dogs, but very mildly seasoned enough only to make them different from McDonald's. Then get the Czech Tourism Ministry to advertise the region as they do other areas of the Czech Republic. Think it will work?"

"That brain of yours never stops going round and round does it?" I teased, "I think it's a great idea, I said you had a social conscience when you came to the hotel the first time, and now I know it's true. You want to help these people, don't you?"

"Don't you?" he inquired with knowing little grin, "Don't pretend to be a hard-ass with me, you are just as taken with them as I am. Now let's go see that room before it's too late to go on today."

The room had 2-double beds and not much more, though the room was large enough for a dresser, a table, a TV, and a comfortable chair. The bathroom dated from the first days of indoor plumbing, but a few innovative changes could make it charmingly old-fashioned European.

A claw-foot-bathtub in excellent condition was the only means of bathing. A new faucet with a shower head attached to a ring suspended from the ceiling, which accommodates a shower curtain, would be inexpensive yet effective. Everything in the room was clean, and in decent condition.

Deciding to stay, we went back to the innkeeper, and told him of our decision, he was elated to have us, it increased his inn's prestige with the mountain people.

What a pleasant night we had with the friendliest, most outgoing, group of partiers I have recently spent an evening with, in college I did have a few of them. The roasted pig was brought upstairs, a huge barrel of beer was hoisted atop the bar, and a spigot affixed.

Villagers started arriving, each carrying their contribution to the feast, sugared yams, fried dumplings, stuffed mushrooms, roasted chestnuts, relishes, pies, cakes, custards, puddings, and dozens of other goodies too numerous to name.

Lexi had an intuition about these people, and he was so right. Some of the men had musical instruments, most of them I'd never seen before, but an accordion showed up on the band shell, and very soon a polka was playing.

The evening air was chilly, but no one seemed to mind, a huge bonfire was burning near the river, and with the strenuous polkas, staying warm was easy.

In the morning, still stuffed from the feast of the previous night, we had coffee, then strolled all the way up the river walk. The river was swollen, and angry looking, a brownish-yellow color with clumps of ice sailing past us.

"Why is there still ice in the river?" I asked Lexi, "And why is it that color?"

"The river begins high up in the mountains; it's fed from the melting ice and snow. There's a lot of water shedding from the snowpack, and it washes soil along with it, that's what the color is,"

As he said that, my attention was diverted to a footbridge 100-feet up stream. Less than 2-feet above the roiling water, a woman pushed a young child from the bridge.

I was in the water before Lexi had a chance to say a word. The water was freezing; the child I figured would be about 30-feet out. I tried to swim a diagonal course to her, but I lost sight of her. I thought she had gone under, in that event it would be all over, the river was too muddy to see anything below the surface.

Just when I was about to give up, she bobbed up again only a few feet from me, I kicked as hard as I could, and managed to get my fingers in her hair. I could feel the cold slowing down my arms and legs, but I managed to turn around, and head for the shore. The shore was different from where I had gone in; I'd been swept down the river to almost past the inn.

I saw Lexi running down the walk to the band shell; he waded out as far as he could go without being swept away himself. The innkeeper, hearing the shouting had come out, and was handing Lexi a long branch of a tree for me to grab, he was there with the branch extended just in time, in two more seconds, the child, and I would have been swept down the river to our deaths.

The pain was excruciating holding onto the branch, my fingers were frozen, my arms, and legs getting weaker by the second. I figured I'd been in the water about 5 or 6-minutes, and if Lexi couldn't pull me out, the cold would finish me off.

I had my left hand on the branch, my right fingers still tangled in the girl's hair. Lexi was pulling me in the direction of the riverbank against the pull of the angry river. The innkeeper got a grip on the branch behind Lexi, with two pulling, I started to move out of the main current, and finally felt my feet touch bottom though there wasn't much feeling left in them.

I stumbled forward, there were arms all over the place, arms grabbing for the little girl, arms grabbing my arms, arms grabbing Lexi, and the innkeeper Tomas. I still don't know where all those people came from, but thankfully they were there.

I saved the little one's life and Lexi saved mine, my mind was swirling like the river, going nowhere fast. I started to fade, but I still heard Lexi barking orders,

"Get the girls clothes off, wrap her up as warm as possible, take her to the kitchen and keep her by the oven, don't use water. Tomas open our room door, and take all the bedding off one bed, and layer it on top of the other bed."

I had no idea what he was yelling, he was speaking Czech. I passed out. He dragged me into our room, and with the help of Tomas got me on the bed, tore my clothes off, and got me under a huge pile of bedding. He

54

tore his own clothes off, climbed into bed with me, both naked, wrapped his arms around me, and started massaging my back, arms, and legs.

Hypothermia is a killer, the blood migrates to the center of the body to protect the vital organs, in severe hypothermia the blood migration cannot be reversed. Moderate hypothermia in a hospital setting is reversed intravenously by warmed liquid pumped through the body's circulating system. In this case, being hours away from a hospital setting was only going to mean emergency action, and luck.

While getting me set up for his personal heat therapy, he instructed Tomas to call Mom in Brno, gave him his cell phone, and told him to hurry.

I was floating aimlessly in space unable to recognize where I was, or where I was going, I'm dead, I told myself, what else could this place be? I couldn't remember how I came to be here, I kept asking no one what happened. Only silence.

An eternity passed with no sight, no sound, and no knowledge of anything. Then I heard a tiny voice say, "Please don't die," and the sound of crying, wracking sobs, my heart ached for the one crying. Another "Please don't die," and some more garbled words I couldn't make out. With only the power of my mind, I moved in the direction of the voice. Then, the voice again, "I love you, please come back."

That was Lexi's voice, who was he speaking to? I strained to hear but there was only muffled sobs. I was suddenly in Lexi's arms he was hugging me, caressing my back and arms and legs, I knew I was in heaven, I had died, I was going to spend eternity like this.

A whispering started in my ear, "Carl, I'm sorry I didn't listen to Dad, he knew I loved you weeks ago, I was afraid to admit it to myself, how could I admit it to you. What you told Dad is the same way I love you, so much it hurts."

He's crying again. Wait, if I'm dead how can I hear him? This must be a dream. Lexi's kissing my lips, eyes, neck and cheeks, I want to kiss him back my lips won't move, I can't open my eyes, this is a fucked up dream. The next dream sequence is Lexi saying,

"I'll do everything I can to make you happy, even get married if that's what you want."

CHAPTER 5

HEROES & LOVERS AT LAST

My body had been sub-zero cold until I heard that, suddenly I felt a flush, as when embarrassed in public, and a wave of heat washes over your body. It calmed me and the dream ended, I slept without anymore dreams.

Waking up, I was shocked to find myself in bed with Lexi, both of us naked. He was staring at me intensely, I panicked and said,

"I broke my promise to you didn't I?"

"No you didn't break your promise; if anyone did, it was me."

"Lexi, I had the strangest dream, you were calling me from faraway asking me not to die, you said you love me and you would do anything to make me happy. even to getting married. That's when I started feeling warm, and the dream ended."

"It wasn't a dream Carl; I was calling you, and begging you not to leave me. I said I love you because I do love you, more than I can express in words, I'll have to show you."

I was in heaven all right but not the same one I thought I was in a while ago. I couldn't believe it had happened so fast, my head was spinning; the whole terrible battle with the river came back to me,

"Where's the little girl," I cried out, "Did she make it? Is she alive? Lexi tell me she's all right. Oh God I'm laying here thinking about myself, and that child needs our help."

Lexi pulled me closer to him, "She's being warmed up by the women from the village, we'll know when Tomas comes back. I gave him my cell phone to call Mom; she might have some answers for us. In the meantime, you aren't leaving this bed I'm not done with you yet."

He kissed me gently on the lips, and in seconds my tongue and his engaged in the age-old dance of love. My hips moved involuntarily, slowly grinding my erection into him, and noticed that he was grinding his into me.

He smelled and tasted so good, I wanted to lick him all over, everywhere, I knew it would taste as good. I'll do that later right now my lips are glued to my Adonis; I don't want to move my tongue to any other location.

We continued grinding, all the while ardently kissing each other, and murmuring moans of pleasure raised to a level that when love is the principal component of the sexual coupling, only then is pleasure truly appreciated.

Our hands found their way to every square-inch of each other's body, nothing has ever felt so seductive, touching, and being touched. Never have my fingers been so sensitive; his skin was silken under my fingertips, smooth, soft, and warm. Lexi groaned and whispered,

"I'm coming Carl."

"I am too Lexi, don't stop."

We climaxed together, our semen coating each other's belly and still we were grinding, and still coming. The bliss ended, but our passion and erections didn't end. We were still in the throes of lovemaking, Lexi turned around, saying,

"I want your semen in my mouth," as he licked the cum off my belly, I licked him clean too, and had him in my mouth in a flash, sucking as if it were the last time I'd be able to, he was doing the same to me, and we came in each other's mouth in just minutes.

I didn't want to stop, my libido or whatever controls our sex drive, was screaming for more of his delicious cum, more of his beautiful sexy body and lips, we still had erections, so he must want more too. Instead of more, he took me gently in his arms, laid me back on the bed, and kissed me tenderly, but with the same ardor as before.

"You had a bad experience and I almost lost you, we're not going to take a chance on a relapse, you need rest. We have all the time in the world to have wonderful hot sex like this 4-times a day every day. Karel, I haven't felt anything close to this, ever."

We fell asleep in each other's arms, his head on my shoulder his lips nuzzling my neck.

We were awakened by a soft rapping on the door, Lexi sat up and pulled on his boxer shorts, "Cone on in it's open," he called, and Tomas came in followed by Dad, "Dad how did you get here?"

"Mom got the mountain extraction team to fly us up in the rescue helicopter; she told them there were two to be extracted, so here we are. Mom and the paramedics are attending to the girl. She may have some mental trauma; it was her mother who pushed her off the bridge. I'll tell you all about it later, right now how is our hero coming along."

Coming and coming and coming, I joked to myself, Dad, you have no idea how right you were.

Aloud, I said, "I'm doing fine, Lexi is my new doctor, he saved my life. Now he won't let me out of bed."

Dad raised an eyebrow, more in the manner of making a statement than questioning, he knows, I thought, that old man has more on the ball than any 3-men half his age.

"Then follow the doctor's orders and stay in bed."

He smiled the same smile that Lexi uses when he's teasing, they're like twins, 40-years apart I thought, I'll never be able to tear this family from my heart, we're stuck with each other.

Five-minutes latter Mom came in wearing a concerned look on her face, she came directly to the bed, leaned over, and kissed my cheek, hesitated, and whispered in my ear,

"You smell interesting, not at all like a patient at deaths door." I felt the blood rushing to my face, she put her cool hand on my forehead, and said to the others, "He's not suffering any problems from the hypothermia, he should take it easy for a day or so, and he'll be as good as new." That was a quick save; no one seemed to notice my blushing.

"The girl will be all right physically, but as I'm sure your father told you, she's sure to have some psychological trouble dealing with such a horrible crime committed on her at such a tender age. It's not just that her mother pushed her from the bridge; it's why she pushed her."

"She caught her husband molesting the child early this morning. She lost it, and stabbed her husband, then she turned on her daughter as the aggressor with her husband. The child fled from the house, the mother caught her on the bridge, and pushed her in the river."

"Several people chased, and caught her on a mountain trail. She told them why she had done such an evil thing, and as soon as the men relaxed, she ran into the forest, they searched, but didn't find her. They looked for the stabbed husband, but couldn't find him either."

My heart was being crushed. Nana and I had eight of these abused children in our foster care, each with a story almost as horrible, each needing love and attention they would never get in any institutional setting.

This one would be no different from those at home, nightmares that froze them immobile, jumping at every sound, and afraid of every shadow. I had to help her, so I asked Mom and Dad,

"I have a team of child psychiatrists for our kids in New York; they deal exclusively with criminally traumatized children." I stated. Before I could continue Lexi chimed in, sounding hurt,

"You have kids? How many kids?"

"They're foster children Lexi, Nana was essentially my babysitter from age two on. When I was thrown out by my father, I took her to my grandparent's house as my guardian; I was only thirteen and would have come under the jurisdiction of the Child Protection Service or in other words, 'foster care'."

"We went to court and had Nana declared my legal Guardian. It's been awhile since I needed a guardian, until this morning," I said smiling at Lexi,

"At sixteen, I was emancipated, I could run my own life, and Nana didn't have much to do. A neighbor couple, who lived next to her parents, friends for years, were killed in a revenge fight that involved the husband. Their 10-year old daughter witnessed the murders, and she shut down completely for more than 6-years,"

"Nana petitioned the CPS and because there were no living relatives they could find, they named Nana as her foster parent. We talked it over, and Nana convinced me that I was in the same category as Rilla, a victim of parental abuse, neglect, or failure to protect their children; we should help children in similar situations."

"For 10-years we have been taking in these damaged little souls, most respond to love and understanding in a few months, but there's some like Rilla who need professional help on a continuing basis."

"Rilla is twenty now, and over her trauma. She helps Nana with the other kids, they love her, she's a real sweet person. We became associated with the psychiatrists when Rilla failed to respond to anyone. Nana knew her since she was born, and it made no difference."

"We have eight children currently living in my grandparent's house, mine now, and five who graduated to life on their own when they were old enough to fend for themselves."

"They still drop in occasionally, and keep us informed of their lives generally, the same as you calling Mom and Dad, they're your anchor, and it's reaffirming to talk every now and then," Mom and Dad were both nodding as I continued, "Is there a way we could relocate this little girl to New York to get the psychiatric help she needs?"

Dad took over, "When there's a medical emergency it's not difficult to get the exit visas, but unless the government doctors rule this a medical problem the visa will be denied."

"It's too early to make a determination on her mental state, some children, like you, are very resilient and manage to heal their own wounds, others are not so strong, it'll be awhile for her to be thoroughly evaluated, I'd say at least 6-months. If you want to file for a visa, I'll do it for you when we get back."

"How do you feel about it Lexi? You're one of her rescuers."

"Carl, you rescued her, I only pulled you out of the water."

"You saved my life; your quick action to warm me up made the difference between my being here and that other place."

"You know that I think you are the bravest person I've ever had the pleasure of knowing you're kind, caring, and full of surprises. Who pays for all these kids?" he asked his voice softening.

"The insurance money initially, and then the charitable trust fund we set up. We have a long trip back, I'll tell you everything about my life, and any other information you want to know."

Dad was listening quietly to our conversation and finally spoke to Lexi, "Son, Carl was not as fortunate as you growing up with a loving family. You know that we've talked on a couple of occasions, it was confidential what he told me, but I can tell you it isn't a pretty picture."

"He did nothing criminal, immoral, or cruel on his part that would make you dislike him. On the contrary, I admire his tenacity to stay above the fray, and cope with some horrible circumstances. If he dumped his story on you all at one time you would think it was fiction, trust me when I tell you it's not."

"Carl had Nana send journals to me from more than 20-years ago, I've been reading them slowly, they are difficult to read and maintain any kind of composure. I will tell you this; we owe Nana a great debt of gratitude for bringing him through this in one piece. Be patient, he'll tell you all, especially now that you've accepted reality. I have to go now, the chopper won't wait forever we've got to get that girl to Brno."

Chapter 6

Cavern behind the falls

After Dad left, Lexi came to sit by me on the bed, and asked me,

"Was it as terrible as Dad made it sound?" I shrugged, unwilling to give my emotions a chance to escape my control.

"Why didn't you at least give me an indication of your past unhappiness? I could have helped you overcome some bad memories."

"I didn't want your pity, I wanted your love."

I answered with my head down, unable to look at him without crying. How did we go from euphoria to depression in such a short time?

"But you have my love," he said as he took my chin in his hand and lifted my head to face him, "If you're suffering I want to know so I can suffer with you, or at least be a comfort to you. Listen to me, I love you. I'm not going to stop because you had a miserable childhood; I'll do everything I can to make our life together seem as if we've achieved Nirvana."

Then he kissed me, we fell back on the bed with our lips locked together, luckily he still had on his shorts and was on top of me when the door opened, and Mom was standing in front of us.

"Well, you two don't waste any time, do you? I came to say good-bye. What I'm witnessing makes me the happiest woman in the world, prayers are indeed answered. We'll be expecting you tomorrow afternoon, we'll have dinner. Give each other a kiss for me."

She breezed out the door the same way she breezed in.

We rolled over facing each other, and started laughing, I told him what she had whispered to me, and we cracked up. Lexi recovered first, and said,

"She's a piece of work isn't she? What mother wants to discover her son having sex with another man? She's not a bad mother, just 50-years ahead of her time."

Stroking each other's backs and butts while we talked, we now got into some heavier groping, and kissing, the passion hadn't diminished one bit, we were as wound up as we were the first time. I never knew that rubbing groins together could be so pleasurable or that it could take you to ejaculation.

Lexi and I learned it together. I think kissing his sensuous mouth was enough to bring on a climatic flood of sperm. With our groins pumping and cocks rubbing together, our passions turned up to maximum heat. We rolled over each other, back and forth, constantly kissing, and nibbling each other's face while whispering vows of love to each other. We climaxed as we had the first time, cleaning each other by licking off each other's sperm, and suckling each other until we ejaculated again in each other's mouth. Lexi took my cock in his hand slowly stroking it,

"I want you to put this in my ass." I was surprised and excited, "If you are inside me we'll be closer to being one, can we try it that way?"

He didn't have to ask twice I rolled his hips up so his sweet hairless ass was staring me in the face. I satisfied another fantasy I had about Lexi; I licked between his ass cheeks and put my tongue on his pulsing little sphincter. The rimming was as erotic as I had dreamed. Many times I had masturbated, fantasizing this act; finally, it was no longer a fantasy.

I enter him a little at a time with his legs over my shoulders, withdrawing and pushing forward again as gently as I could. He made no complaint that it hurt, and he maintained his erection. After a few more thrusts and withdrawals, we were moving in unison, he took me in as far as I could go. I started pumping my hips faster, he cried,

"Fuck me Carl, you feel so good inside me."

I leaned forward and kissed him on the lips, twisting our tongues together never missing a beat. He was clenching his sphincter and releasing it in time to my inward thrusts. I could feel an ejaculation building in my scrotum, it was tightening. My groin was on fire, it erupted, I came, fully embedded inside my gorgeous lover, he was moaning with pleasure and masturbating.

I placed my hand on his cock, and finished the job for him; he came, calling my name as he flooded his chest and stomach with semen. I withdrew from him, and immediately had his penis in my mouth eating the last of the sweet, hot sperm leaking from it, then licked it from his stomach and chest.

I fell on him exhausted, I could swear he was purring, or was it coming from me?

We slept for an hour, when I awoke; Lexi was on one elbow his head in his hand looking down at me with such a loving look that I was almost ready to orgasm again.

"Are you hungry lover, for something other than sex? I think we should make an appearance in the barroom before they think we're dead. Let's take a quick bath together, then go up to the bar."

The bathtub was not meant for two, but we managed to cavort and fondle each other while washing, it was the most intimate time outside of bed I could imagine.

A little past noon we got to the barroom, the place was full.

"So much for lunch," Lexi muttered.

The door hadn't even closed behind us when a loud cheer rolled over us. We were surrounded at once, lifted up onto the bar where two glasses of beer were thrust at us. Every person there raised his or her own beer in a toast, yelling something in Czech. Lexi raised his glass and yelled over the din, 'na zdravi', the crowd roared and yelled 'na zdravi' back at him, turned their glasses up and emptied them, so we did as well.

They repeated it three more times, and it got me feeling woozy from the beer. Lexi held up both hands palms out to the crowd, they quieted, and he said, 'Dekuji', which sounded like 'dack wee', they started shouting like a chant, "Hrdina, Hrdina, Hrdina. I managed to get Lexi's attention and signaled my bewilderment, he cupped his hand around my ear, and told me they were yelling, hero, hero, hero. I was caught unawares; adulation was never something I craved, especially when it involved saving the life of a child. I put my hands around my mouth and yelled,

"No, No" They went wild, "Why are they cheering?" I asked Lexi,

"You told them yes, not, no."

Damn, I forgot that 'no' means 'yes' and 'yes' means 'no' in Czech, so I tried again,

"Ano, ano." They shouted back, "No, no."

The beer and the language reversing was confounding me, I asked Lexi to stop them, they were wrong I was no hero.

"Would you have me try to stop a runaway train?" He yelled, "I'll try."

He held out his hands again and they responded respectfully. He spoke to them for several minutes, all the heads turned to me with sympathetic expressions on their faces. Two men stepped up to the bar, each took me by an arm and lifted me to the floor, they pulled a chair over, and gently sat me as if I were so fragile I'd break.

A booming voice caused the crowd to part and make way for Tomas, carrying two platters heaped with sausage, sauerkraut, buttered beets, and boiled potatoes. Lexi sat; Tomas placed a loaf of freshly baked bread between us, and asked a serving girl to bring us beer.

The situation was comical in which no was laughing. People surrounded our table and stared at us while we ate. Watching paint dry would be more interesting, but rather disconcerting when you're the one trying to eat.

We were hungry enough to manage to stuff ourselves to the approval of the crowd, which cheered again when we finished eating. Lexi addressed them again and everyone found a seat. He pulled up a chair beside him and because the crowd believed I was an invalid, or injured, I sat down.

For the next hour, Lexi conducted a town meeting with the dexterity of a seasoned politician. As outraged over the woman's actions as they were, they answered questions, and gave their opinions in an orderly and polite manner.

I knew he was gathering material for our plan of action in the very near future. He had the knack of getting people to do his bidding by getting them to suggest what he wanted them to do.

He organized them into search parties after getting their input on areas virtually impassable, and areas most likely having hiding places, such as caves, or hidden ravines. When a likely area was mentioned, and heads nodded knowingly, Lexi would prompt them to suggest a way to search the area, and how many men it would take.

The party broke up when Lexi told them we had to do it today so we could be back for the nights festivities. We pressed two strapping farmers to go with Lexi and me to the house where the woman supposedly had stabbed her husband.

The river walk ran up to the footbridge where the angry river still boiled like a cauldron around the piers. Past the ramp to the bridge was only a dirt path following the river up to a large ravine.

About 400-feet past the bridge, sitting on a good-sized lot, overgrown with scrub oak and laurel was a barely standing once productive little farm. The house was now so neglected that it hardly even qualified as housing.

We went inside the tiny 2-room structure, the stench was breathtaking. This disaster only happened early this morning, the condition of this pig sty existed before the attempted murder.

Looking around, we worried about touching anything, the place was so filthy. One main room for cooking and living, a small alcove with a pallet made of some unknown material was the parent's sleeping area, and a loft over it with enough room for a child to sleep.

On the floor beside the pallet was a once white, robe like garment, a death head crudely drawn on it with charcoal. I pointed it out to Lexi, and he showed the two farmers. When they looked at it, the older one's eyes bulged; he made a strangled sound in his throat, and went in reverse, back out the door way past the speed limit. He was nowhere in sight when I got to the door.

Lexi caught the younger one's arm and was pulled outside of the house by his urgent need to put some distance between him and this place. The man could hardly talk he kept telling Lexi, evil, devil, evil, he disappeared back down the dirt path.

We found no body, or even blood that we could see; no blood outside the house or on the trail. If the husband were stabbed there should be some evidence of bleeding.

Back at the Inn, we cornered Tomas, who seemed the most levelheaded of the villagers. Lexi described the robe we had seen, Tomas blanched, his voice quavered, and one word escaped his lips, 'Satanists'.

It seems we had been on the wrong track, these people were terrified, not of living/dead vampires, but living fanatics, terrorizing the superstitious villagers. We planned to leave in the morning the next day, but decided to do a little investigating, leave around noon, and be at Mom and Dads house by late afternoon.

Word had spread of our finding the robe, and the villagers cowered in their homes, believing evil forces were about to strike the bucolic village.

The 5-day celebration of May Day was apparently over, as no one showed up at the inn. Tomas was not bothered by the cancelation; he told Lexi that it was better, large gatherings may be a target for the evil ones.

He was clearly frightened out of his wits, but wouldn't tell us why, and more information about who these evil ones were, was not forthcoming.

He served us a cold supper of local goat milk cheese, warm slabs of bread slathered with homemade butter, and slices of a salami type sausage, pleasantly spiced with garlic and I think, fennel.

These people may not be sophisticated gourmets, but they could serve a most satisfactory meal. We washed down the food with the ever present beer (I don't think they believe in drinking water), and retired to our room, pleasantly exhausted from the activity of the past couple of hours, and our marathon lovemaking.

Despite our exhaustion sex reared its wondrous head, or heads, and we took each other in our mouths again, and as before were very quickly feeding our semen to each other, we stayed that way for minutes. I was reluctant to end the most satisfying sex I've ever experienced with another man. I was shamelessly in love with my Lexi.

We slept wrapped in each other's embrace, and woke to bright sunlight filling the room's window. Despite our engorged sex organs, and the pleasurable feel of our bodies pressing close to each other, we left the bed with reluctance, performed our morning hygiene, dressed, and headed for the inn.

Tomas served us a bowl of porridge like substance with a taste and texture between farina and grits, gut warming, and filling, spiced with cinnamon and nutmeg.

Tomas was still reticent about the robe, so we dropped the subject and questioned him about the path past the footbridge. Where did it lead? Would we be trespassing if we continued up the ravine? Most important, were there any hidden dangers that we should know about?

The path led to a bluff, or meadow, back pastures along the top of the ravine, apparently for community farms to use.

A waterfall was at the far end of the ravine. A farmer was not allowed to own water rights, considered a common necessity for the community. We wouldn't be trespassing, and the only danger was that the waterfall was haunted.

The layers of superstition and fear were getting crazier by the day, but it was intriguing, it made us more interested and eager to investigate what was happening to these good people.

We set out up the river walk, passed the bridge, and walked down the small incline until we were only a few inches from the swollen river. The path continued on the same level as the river for about a mile, then forked off to a path that rose at a 25-degree incline for approximately 500-feet to level off 100-feet above the fork.

The other fork continued up the river, but was narrower now because of the increasingly high sides of the ravine, we could hear the thunder of the waterfall long before we saw it; a sharp turn to the right suddenly brought it into view.

What a view it was, a crescent shaped cataract easily 200-foot wide and at least 100-foot high, was no more than 50-feet in front of us. It must have been an optical illusion because both of us stopped dead in our tracks as if we might fall into the curtain of water cascading so close to us.

The roar of the water was deafening, Lexi was trying to tell me something, but it was impossible to hear. He tapped my shoulder and pointed to the sandy soil of the path where the spray from the falls had wet it. Grooves in the sand very clearly visible, caused no doubt, by something being dragged, a body perhaps, the grooves made by the feet.

The grooves ran to within 10-feet of the water and because a rock ledge ran from there into the waterfall, the drag marks vanished. Lexi motioned me forward and took my hand; I realized that he believed the ledge was a walkway behind the falls, and we were about to go in.

I had no wish to plunge into that energy sapping frigid shower, but if partners share the work and the rewards, they must also share the risks.

With our backs pressed firmly against the wall of the ravine, we inched our way into the thick mist roiling in our faces. No actual water was falling on us, just the much moisturized mist, which wet us to the skin in seconds.

My intrepid lover pulled me with him inch by inch until we were standing in a blind. A rock wall jutting from inside the falls hid the space behind it, even when the volume of water was much lower this wall would appear to block any means of going behind the waterfall. A narrow space on the rock ledge allowed us to snake around the blind

We found ourselves in a cavern; on the opposite side there was a faint glimmer of daylight that indicated a possible entrance on the other side of the river. The roof disappeared into blackness as did the back of the cavern, in the dim light I reckoned it to be somewhere around 80 to 90-foot wide. A little damp for any creature to make it their home, so there was no fear of running into a 4-legged creature, but a 2-legged one is another story.

The dampness in the cave and my wet clothes gave me a good excuse to pull Lexi back to the entrance; he wanted to leave as badly as I it seemed. We inched our way out faster than going in.

Exiting the icy shower we noticed an extra set of footprints in the wet sand, they were coming and going. Around the sharp turn there was no sign of anyone on the path, which was nearly impossible for someone to get down that long narrow canyon to the fork in the short time we were in the cave. Whoever it was had disappeared.

We walked soaking wet back to the inn; Tomas saw us and asked Lexi,

"Did you go back in the river?"

"We found a cave behind the waterfall do you know about it?"

Tomas trembled, "You didn't go in did you? That's a bad place, bad things happen there. You are nice boys I don't want anything bad to happen to you."

Lexi tried to avoid alarming him, "What bad things happen there Tomas?"

"Torture, mutilation, death and much more," He was scared, and he was more worried for us than for himself. We talked him down from his near hysteria and decided to leave the rest for now.

We left for our room to clean up and get into some dry clothes, it was afternoon already, and we had a long slow ride back to Brno.

Tomas refused to accept payment from us for the room, or the food and drink,

"We owe you much more than a little money, I think you two started to bring people together again, you showed us courage and bravery that had all but disappeared in these mountains. I wish you could stay and help us face our fears, people yesterday reminded me of how we were a long time ago."

"We're coming back, Tomas, you can tell everyone that we're going to talk to government agencies to see about improving your roads, and fixing the electrical distribution system for two examples. You told me there's a line coming in here across the mountain from Olomouc, right? Well one line's not very efficient or reliable; it must be taken care of for River Town, and all the other villages in this part of the Carpathians."

We left Tomas with a relieved look on his grinning face, and carried our luggage back to the car down by the band shell. Even before we got to the car Lexi knew something was wrong,

"What's that on the hood of the car?" he asked me, "Looks like an animal."

We approached the car and saw Tomas' old dog, dead on the hood of our car with a slit throat. Tomas was devastated,

"I knew something bad would happen, they know every move we make, they watch us every minute. Do you understand why the villagers are nervous? Boys this is just a warning, they don't want you here, they sense you may change things."

"Tomas, they're not going to scare us away. Think about this; if someone is watching all the time, it must be by someone who lives in the village, or near enough to be known, there's no strangers hanging around is there?"

"No, I see what you're trying to say, these Satanists are living among our people,"

"They are your people, evil people are everywhere. You can't find them because they appear to be regular people. They're undermining everything that's good and decent, causing exactly what's happening to your village now."

"Fear, suspicion, and superstition are the goals of these Satanists, and they think they're winning. The husband that was supposedly stabbed, did you know him?"

"Of course I knew him, I didn't like him, he was a bully and a drunk."

"Did he have any friends, especially any he associated with a lot? Lexi asked, planting the idea for Tomas to start watching for watchers.

"A couple, also bullies, I've had to throw them out of my barroom many times for causing trouble. I'm going to keep an eye on them."

"Good," Lexi said beaming like a teacher who just got through to a student, "While we're gone think about who else might fit the picture of a Satanist, but keep it to yourself, if they get the idea that we're on to them they might hurt you, or worse shut you up permanently. We're going to report this to the constable to have a record of it at least."

"Don't do that, after what you told me I think he may be one of them, he's friends with one of the two I told you about. Let's not let them know it bothers us, it might slow them down."

I know Lexi didn't believe it, but we we're leaving, and that might have the same result.

Chapter 7

A Stradivari sings again

On the way to Brno he told me what Tomas had said, I told him of my frustration that I can't converse with them in their language, Lexi pointed out,

"Even if you learn Czech you'll have a difficult time conversing with them. They speak a dialect that originated when Romania was the dominant power in the Carpathians. Throw in a little Slovak and some Polish, and you'll be able to talk with them. I've spoken Czech all my life and I have a hard time understanding everything they say, I wing it a lot."

He keeps saying things like that in such an unabashed way that endears him to me even more.

"Lexi, you said Tomas told you that electricity is brought in over the mountains from Olomouc. Why is that the best way?" I asked.

"Because it would be about 80-kilometers longer to bring it in from Hodonin," he replied as if I should know that.

"I didn't mean running 100-miles of electric lines, you're an Electrical Engineer didn't you see that waterfall? Isn't Hydroelectric in your area of expertise?"

"Carl you clever devil, I was so into those assholes making trouble, that I never thought of the potential of the falls, you are so right that alone would be a huge economic plus for the area. I'm wondering now if any studies have been done to measure seasonal flow, that's something else we can check out."

"A couple of generators could produce a half-million-kilowatts, that's more than enough for every village up here, the excess could be transmitted back down the line they use now to bring it in, or extend the transmission lines into Slovakia. You, my love are a genius."

We were late. Mom was frantic; Dad was cool as always but worried underneath. They hugged and kissed us as if we'd been missing for months. Lexi, to get a rise out of them, explained,

"We had to bury Tomas' dog after it got its throat slit."

It worked, Mom let out a strangled 'What'? Dad was a little less shocked than Mom, but his expression was very similar. We explained everything that had happened after they left, except the best parts, our sexual romps.

They weren't overly shocked; it was a common occurrence in the mountains. Most of it stemmed from resentment of those trapped in their circumstances, and got sucked into cults that promised a better life than they were living. When the cult descended into hate and debauchery, it would be too late. The shame of it is that no one cares until a crime is committed, there's nothing anyone can do about it.

They agreed we should try to help them anyway we could. Dad made a suggestion that when we go back up there, we take a few battery operated miniature cameras placed to see anyone following us when out digging up information.

Mom had an idea of opening a clinic once a month for women's health issues. Being able to talk one on one would possibly get one at least, to open up about the frightening events that have the populace so terrified.

Then Dad torpedoed the chit chat,

"Mom tells me you two were in a compromising position when she went to say good-bye, have I a son-in-law, or are you experimenting?"

Lexi was so confident of his parent's love that he didn't experience a minute's embarrassment, and spoke up for both of us,

"It took almost losing him to realize how much I love him, I've indulged in gay sex a couple of times, not because I curious, but to understand how it would be if I admitted I'm gay.

I hated the lifestyle not the sex; Carl showed me it doesn't have to be that way. He's more a man than the straight kids I grew up with, if you don't approve of him I'll just have to leave and never see you again."

They knew he was joking and Mom slapped him on his arm and came back with, "You go ahead and leave we'll keep Carl here."

Dad reached over and squeezed my hand, "I guess I've got a son-in-law." Tears all around, a happy ending to long sad movie.

Mom finally herded us into the kitchen with her complaints that the dinner was ruined. That wasn't the case; it was delicious, as all her meals are. We ate and enjoyed the banter of a close family.

Dad changed the mood by asking me,

"Carl I've read your journals, and I'd like to have your permission to discuss this with Lexi and Mom present. We should have no secrets among us, as I expected back in April, you two would eventually get together."

"As traumatic as the circumstances were I'm glad it happened sooner, you were torturing yourselves, and it's obvious to Mom and me that you love each other, and have for quite a while I think. Is it all right with you?"

"I promised Lexi that I'd tell him everything, if Mom wants to hear it then I'm okay with it."

Dad gave them the main points of what I had related to him in April, both looked incredulous,

"I know it sounds unbelievable, that's because you're hearing it second hand if you heard it from his mouth, you wouldn't be so skeptical."

He took out a couple of journals and read entries from my past, everything he read confirmed what he had related to them. They lost their incredulous expressions and replaced them with looks of distaste at the pain they were hearing from his reading.

"What I've read you is a mere introduction to a cruelty we will never understand. These journals are very difficult reading, not due to poor writing, but to the gut-wrenching content of the dialogue."

"Carl is a very wealthy man; by his estimate he inherited several hundred million dollars when he was thirteen. The house on Fifth Avenue was the only thing he wanted, to get away from his father. The rest was in a trust fund until he reached his majority at eighteen."

"His grandparents had set up a college fund he could access at any age. Money was the bane of his existence. he didn't want it; it was because of money that his mother had left."

"At thirteen he had no one except his au pere, or sitter, or guardian as she was finally granted by the courts. I called her in New York as she requested, to confirm the receipt of the journals."

"Her name is Betty Cavendish; she was hired to be Carl's nanny when he was two. Due to her perseverance, Carl is with us today, and is the fine young man we know him to be. I'm sure Carl doesn't want me to recite a long list of injuries and unjustified verbal assaults, so I'm going to give the one that drove our maestro from his father's house."

"He told me he had a piano teacher and a violin teacher; I asked him if he could play either, and he replied, 'both'. We heard him at the piano; we agree he can play it,"

"I've told you of the shameful treatment by his father relating to Juilliard. I couldn't know or judge the truthfulness of his story, only what was in the journals. Was the story exaggerated? Was he embellishing the correspondence from Juilliard?"

"Unanswered questions until I found an envelop in the journals. The demo CD he had sent to the school was in the envelope with two letters, I think you should read them."

Dad handed the reply from Juilliard to Mom, she read it, and handed it to Lexi, he handed her the note my father had slipped in the reply letter.

Mom is a very controlled lady, a lady in every sense of the word, she read the note, and the three of us almost fell off our chairs as she hollered the loudest I've heard her voice,

"What a fucking prick."

Lexi snatched the note from her hand and read the note; tears were streaming down his face, unable to make a response.

"The letter from Juilliard states they had reason to believe the demo was 'enhanced' in a studio," Dad started in again, "I have no idea what enhanced would sound like, I do know that it's a very excellent rendition of 'Brahms Violin Concerto in E Major'."

"I took the liberty of playing the demo for the conductor of the Prague Philharmonic Orchestra, his first comment was 'that's a Stradivari' I told him you had told me it was. Then, 'who is this virtuoso'?"

"I told him your name, he said,"

"I've never heard of him."

"I told him the story, and he was skeptical."

"It's an incredible tale to be sure," he said, "Why don't you bring him around and let me see him play the same piece, he can even use my Stradivari? I can't believe that was the performance of a 13-year-old."

"I asked him if Saturday afternoon was a good time, and he said it would be perfect. So can we keep the appointment?"

Lexi spoke up, "Carl, say 'yes' please, for me. Show them the truth."

"Will he tell me if my demo was enhanced or tampered with? I wouldn't put anything past my father."

"I'm sure that's why he wants to see you play."

"On a Stradivari?"

"That's what he said,"

"Okay, I'd love to play a Stradivari again. I hope we're all going, you'll love the sound of an instrument singing."

Saturday arrived, my stomach was churning, I hadn't even seen a violin after leaving mine behind in the great escape. I thought that if the piano came back so easily, so would the violin. The conductor lived in a wealthy suburb of Brno only 10-minutes from Mom and Dad's house. We were shown into the Maestro's office by his assistant and had introductions all around.

"I'm pleased to meet you Carl, if Ivan's estimation of you is real, then you are one in a million. Do you know who we are?"

"The Prague Symphony, you're famous worldwide, Gustav Mahler premiered his symphony number seven here, conducting the orchestra himself."

"Excellent, you know then that we are a professional organization. Will you accept my critique of your performance?"

"Maestro, I haven't played in 13-years, I'll give it my best try, I want to disprove the suspicion that my demo was 'enhanced' in a studio. Your critique is welcome, good, or bad."

"Then have at it," the Maestro grinned, handing me a violin case.

"What a lovely instrument," I managed to get out, when I saw the Stradivari nestled in its bright-red cocoon, "Are you sure it's okay to play this delicate antique?"

"The fact that you recognize it as a delicate antique makes it okay, it was made for playing."

I tuned the violin a bit, it must have been played recently, the strings had good tension.

"The first movement is mostly orchestra; I'm going to start at the second-movement, which is the same as the demo about 20-minutes."

I placed the instrument under my chin, and was transported instantly backward in time 13-years; it felt as if the Stradivari were part of me. As I prayed it might be, the ability had not deserted me.

I played the opening phrases tentatively to see whether I was going to fail. As my confidence grew, so did my passion, and soon I was so immersed in the concerto that time ceased to exist, and only the singing of the violin was reality.

I finished and brought the violin across my chest as I was taught all those years ago, there was silence in the room, and I didn't know how to interpret it. Lexi broke the silence by jumping from his chair, and took the violin away from me,

"Carl," he almost shouted, "Your fingers are bleeding, someone give me a towel."

The room came alive, the Maestro's assistant handed Lexi a towel that he used to wipe the blood from my fingers, and wrap it around my hand. I watched him do it with a stupid expression on my face, as if I didn't know why he was doing that.

Mom came to me, and put her arms around me as if I really were thirteen again. I could feel her love pouring over me, it wasn't pity it was more chagrin at the disappointment and humiliation that had plagued my life.

Lexi was still holding my hand, I felt no pain in my hand only the warmth he sent through the towel, he whispered in my ear,

"I didn't think I could love you more than I did this morning, but I do."

The Maestro and Dad had been talking quietly at the Maestro's desk, the assistant was signaled to come over, and they had their heads together for a couple of minutes talking in low, but intense voices.

Dad looked up at me, "Carl, don't get angry with what I'm about to tell you,"

Mom, Lexi, and I thought my recital was going to be panned, and I guess our faces showed it.

"It's not what you think; the performance was stellar, brilliant. The Maestro tells me he knows several violin virtuosos who can't master that concerto."

"I wanted to tell you I agreed to let them videotape your recital, primarily to compare the sound tracks. That was out the window early; your CD was not 'enhanced'. The Maestro now wants to know why the director of Juilliard would say such a thing without doing what we did here today, meaning a live audition."

"He wants to e-mail the video to the director, whom he knows very well, to get an explanation of why he would suppress such talent. Especially in one so young and claim you had no passion or technical expertise."

"Thirteen-years with no practice or mentoring, and you have passion not seen very often, about technical expertise; you could teach it to most veterans of the symphony. Do you mind if he sends the video to the director?"

"Only if the director honors my request that my father knows nothing of this, and he never sees the video." I stated.

"I'm sure it will be no problem," the Maestro said, "Jon is an honorable man that is why I want to hear his explanation. I'll extract a promise from him about your father, I'm certain he will understand."

With that said, the assistant, who proofed the tape, transferred the file to his e-mail address, and sent it to New York, with a message to call as soon as he had viewed the video, and included my conditions.

CHAPTER 8

THE 600 POUND GORILLA

I gave them my theory regarding why the director wrote that letter of rejection when we were in the car again,

"My father is a patron of the arts, supposedly; he really doesn't give a damn for anything but making money. His patronage is done for tax reasons; I'll bet Juilliard receives a healthy donation every year. If he threatened to withdraw his funding, the director would be forced to throw me under the bus."

"That sounds plausible," Dad said, "It's a shame that money trumps all."

Mom joined the discussion by recalling what Dad had read to them, "His anger at you was probably heightened considerably when you told him you didn't want his money that would seem to him, a sacrilege."

"Your father is a seriously disturbed psychopath, there's no other explanation why a man would damage his own son to avenge a perceived wrong Carl," she said as she stroked my hair, "We're not going to let anything like that hurt you again, I know Lexi feels that way too, so does Dad. I just want to tell you that if he were here now, I'd strangle him. Did he hound you after he threw you out of the house?"

"No, not directly anyway, he stopped all payments to my tutors, Nana and my bodyguards, the music teachers were dismissed before he told me to get out, and I had given up on that endeavor anyway. Nana thought he had a responsibility to pay for my education, and we should sue him. I rejected that idea, I didn't want his money."

"We went to the trustees and got them to release funds from my education trust fund with no problem, so he didn't get any satisfaction from his petty, vengeful act."

"At fourteen, I took the PSAT tests for entrance to a community college, NYU wouldn't accept me, I was too young. At sixteen, I was old enough and transferred to the 4-year school, majored in Journalism and English and got two BAs just after my seventeenth birthday."

"I had studied creative writing at the community college; it had been almost a compulsion to write long before college, as Dad probably deduced from my journals. I wrote articles for many magazines and my published rate was above 80% that turned out to be a good record."

"I didn't realize they were a magazine publishing house, publishing many magazines. They knew me even if I didn't know it; by nineteen, I was employed by them."

"I supported myself on my earnings, and was self-sufficient, the only exception was the town house, we had Rilla living there by then, and a couple of other kids, so I couldn't walk away from it. I figured the good we were doing for these kids overrode my desire to distance myself from it completely."

"The only thing I still have to make you aware of, in the spirit of full disclosure, is my true worth. At eighteen I met with my grandparent's lawyers for the disposition of the will, which I had never paid any attention to."

"I was told of the NY real estate and the town house with its own maintenance fund that they had put in my name for some inexplicit reason and thought that was it."

"At the meeting they informed me that cash, T notes, certificates of deposit, bonds, stocks, mutual funds, hedge funds, and more that I can't remember, was at last through probate court. 70% inheritance taxes and outrageous lawyer's fees all paid. I am worth 1.5-billion dollars."

Before anyone could reply I went on, "You might think that would be good news, it wasn't. For several years Nana and I had been giving away money at a furious rate, to every charity we could find that didn't keep 90% of donations to pay themselves huge bonuses every year. So many con artists and thieves are in the charity business, it's hard to know who to trust."

"We researched dozens of charities and nonprofit organizations, in most of them the negatives outweighed the positive results of their altruism. I wanted to do worthwhile things with the money, and do it responsibly; I had my own lawyers by then and had everything, including the town house, put into an untraceable blind trust. My name appears nowhere except in the legal documents, and that's shielded from the public record."

"Then we set up our own foundations, no more than 20% of the yearly endowments could be taken for administrative costs, including salaries. Nana and I took no salary, and we were not compensated for our time at all."

"No executive committee meetings in Aspen or Acapulco, we tried to pare the waste so those who needed the charity the most, were not shortchanged by people who only worked for the charity for their own benefit."

"Before the discovery of even greater wealth, we had set up several organizations; a battered women's shelter, an abused children's fund, an animal rescue fund, the Wheelchair-bound foundation, and disabled vets aid. We gave generously to worthy groups like; Save the Whales, Returning Vets, and others."

"Afterward, it seemed such a fool's errand, even giving away millions, the trust fund was gaining ground on us, income on investments after taxes-and we didn't take deductions for charitable donations-was more than we had given away."

"I changed the way I thought about the very rich, and became more determined than ever to rid myself of this curse. Nana works exclusively on setting up foundations, we have more than a hundred now, and we fund them for 10-year intervals."

"It's reduced the trust fund quite a bit, but it's also making money hand over fist. Three more, honest caring people would help us enormously. I'll shut up now."

Lexi, looking troubled responded first,

"Carl, I feel intimidated by such a large amount of money; it sort of makes you the 600-pound gorilla in the room."

"I figured there would be some bad feelings about this, and I've been trying to resolve the problem. Here's what we can do; go to New York, we marry, I give you my love and half of the money, you give me your love, and take half the money, we'll both be 300-pound gorillas."

Dad cracked up, Mom, getting the meaning of my proposal, did too. Lexi wasn't very amused,

"Don't joke about it, I don't want anything to come between us, especially not money."

"I'm not joking, and it wouldn't come between us if we were in identical positions. Since you've known me have I ever talked about money except what we earn? I didn't lie to you about money I said I lived on what I earn and that's the truth. Lexi, I don't want the money, I want you."

"If I gave it to anyone who asked, or let people cheat and steal it, greedy people, who are going to blow it on themselves and end up broke what would you think of me?"

"I'd think you were crazy and irresponsible, okay I get your point, but is giving half to me the only way to resolve this?"

"If we want to be 300-pound gorillas together, then yes. I told you my name doesn't appear on any documents except the blind trust declaration, it's shielded, and yours will be too. No one has so much as mentioned a handout because I put everything in trust."

"Before I did that I constantly had calls, asking for money, or pretending to be holding the patent on some fabulous invention. They needed me to invest a couple of million dollars to develop this marvel, schemes, and scams over and over."

"However many times we changed our phone number they always found the new one, it only slowed them for a day. Six-years ago, we changed the number for the last time, unlisted like the others, but no dollar signs after the name meant no interest."

Dad took control of the conversation, "Lexi, Carl is offering you a compromise three-quarters of the world would jump at, what I think we missed is what Carl said a minute ago, Lexi didn't bat an eyelash, nor did Mom, am I the last to know?"

"About what dear," Mom asked with feigned innocence, "Didn't I tell you, Lexi and Carl are going to be married?"

"It must have slipped your mind, such an insignificant, unimportant bit of news," he joked ironically.

"Ivan, I just learned about it the same time you did, Lexi obviously knew about it-dah" she mocked, "I don't care how we found out, I'm thrilled that it's going to happen, aren't you?"

We arrived back at the house, but the discussion was far from over, even walking in the door, they were still bantering.

"Barbara, how many times have we discussed this? We agreed to not go overboard when he finally found himself, now you're going overboard."

Lexi trying to be stern interjects a, "Hey, I'm right here, stop talking like that. How long have you known I was gay?"

Mom pretended to think, "About the same time Carl's father knew, there's little signs along the way if you care to read them, they start at birth, a newborn has sexuality, it's the human condition."

"The great debate over nurture or nature is out of sync, its not nurture, or nature its nurture *and* nature, every human, and probably animals too have a mix of male and female genes, a preponderance of male genes let's say, will ensure testosterone saturated, heterosexual men."

"As the male gene level falls, the male has higher level of estrogen than his macho counterpart, and is not as 'manly'. Continue down the scale, and you find very effeminate men, and what are called Nellie queens."

"At the bottom is the hermaphrodite with an even split of male and female genes, and, consequently, has both male and female reproductive organs."

"Up the other side of the curve is higher testosterone, and lower estrogen, evidenced by facial hair, smaller breasts, and heavier body mass. Going up the scale, the more female genes, the more womanly, until the ultimate highest level of female genes gives us 'Playboy bunnies', and swim wear models or 'all woman' types. We all fit on the curve somewhere; we have no control over it."

"Man has tried for millennia to change the nature we were endowed with, there has there never been a period in the history of man that didn't have men attracted to other men, and women who slept with other women."

"Every religion has condemned it since the beginning of history, has it made any difference? No it hasn't, you can't change nature, not with threats of death, imprisonment, beatings, electrical shock therapy, or prayer."

"We are what nature has made. To try not to be as nature dictates is a recipe for pain or suffering caused by betrayal, not only of the hurt spouse and children, but also by betrayal of your own nature to begin with."

"To understand is to let your child develop in his own way at his own pace, societal pressure is part of the equation, but in the end nature triumphs. Lexi, you are the living proof of my theory. Dad and I decided a long time ago that you would most likely be gay, we agreed not to interfere with nature, and let you be whoever you would be."

"It's no surprise to us that you love Carl, he's like you except you have blond hair and blue eyes, he has black hair and green eyes. You're on the curve at the same point, I guess, and the attraction for each other is overwhelmingly strong."

"Now, tell me when and where, this will happen, you can do it here now, but there are a few restrictions, such as you won't be able to adopt children, and it's called Registered Partnerships, not marriage."

"Although the most liberal in the EU, it has a long way to go to full equality. Perhaps New York would be a better choice; you'd have all the rights accorded to any other married couple."

"They are going to decide that themselves Barbara," Dad told her, "We should butt out and let them do what they think is best for them."

"That's fine with me as long as we're invited." Mom replied, "Carl how are your fingers?"

"They'll be fine, if I'm ever going to play the violin again I'll have to get the calluses back on my fingers, the strings are murder on uncallused skin."

"We had better start right away; you're going to play again, even if it's only for me. I heard the violin sing, Carl, I got lost in the music, and didn't want it to stop; it felt as if you were playing for me. What a great gift you have, I don't have any problem if you share that one with me."

Dad agreed, "My wish is that the world would be able to share it Lexi, it's selfish to keep the music for a select audience."

"I'm not sure what I want to do, getting to be proficient on the violin again will take many hours of practice, there are many other things I want to do, and spending hours at a time perfecting just one small difficult passage isn't it. Lexi, I'll play for you anytime you want me to, but we have much work to do in the mountains, we're not giving up on that dream, or giving up on the people up there."

"Exactly what is it you're planning to do?" Dad asked, "How can Mom and I help?"

"Dad you are helping, you guys are doing the hard part trying to get information from the bureaucracy that by itself saves us hours of leg work, where we can be doing things that might be dangerous for you to do."

Lexi was a little condescending I thought, so a little humor might help, "Yeah, like crawling through a waterfall with a million tons of water pouring around your ears."

Mom was horrified, "You don't mean to tell me that you risked your lives going into a waterfall?"

"It's not that risky, obviously someone else had been there, dragging something, probably the body right up to the water, we didn't run in like gangbusters, we were very cautious, and went very slowly, and got very wet."

"A huge cavern is behind the falls, it was too dark to see anything, but enough lambent light to know it's a big space, we're planning to go back with lights."

Dad this time sounding concerned, "If it looked as if someone dragged a body into the falls," he said, "How is that not risky Lexi? You didn't know whether someone was in there, and could attack you, or shoot both of you."

"The husband's body is the only possible 'dragee' that happened the day before; the cave is not a place to linger for more than 24-hours. When we go back there we'll be wearing slickers, have many people with us for protection, and lots of electric candlepower." I said to calm his alarm.

Lexi the diplomat changed the subject, "Carl could we set up a 'Foundation for the electrification of River Town' to pay for the exploratory work and move it along a little faster?"

"As I said before, that brain of yours never stops turning, that's a good idea, and you're right, it'll save time. I'll call Nana and get her on it tomorrow, well, maybe Monday. Something else I was wondering about, is there a way we could use that cavern for the machinery?"

"I want to check that out when we get back to Prague. We have a couple of weeks before the publisher's submission requirements, but we're probably cutting it close. So if you pound out an article about the mountains, I'll go talk to a professor who worked in Hydro Electrical production before he retired to teach."

"I'll stop at the Ministry of Natural Resources first to see if there's a study for seasonal flow on that river. Mountain River and the Morava feed the Danube, the Danube doesn't dry up in summer, so this river is most likely active all year, which means a viable source of hydroelectric power."

We ate dinner and had a pleasant evening reminiscing about Lexis's childhood here in Brno at this wonderful house. We retired early, mainly to play before sleeping, and went to my room.

The door hadn't had time to close before Lexi jumped on me, carrying the two of us onto the bed, his hot mouth was over mine kissing me as if we hadn't kissed in days. Without taking our lips apart for more than a few seconds to pull our T-shirts off, we clumsily worked to take our pants off, and almost tore each other's underwear off. In a husky voice, he whispered in my ear,

"Don't move."

He proceeded to kiss my neck, chest, and my nipple, which he gently bit and scraped with his teeth, my nipples were as hard as my cock. He was fondling my other nipple, rolling it between his fingers, my body was on fire, I wanted him to take me in his mouth. I felt such an urgency to couple with him, but he was making love not just having sex.

With his fingers of one hand still fondling my nipple, his other hand went down between my legs and began caressing my inner thigh. Each caress sent shivers of lust into my groin, his lips moved down to kiss my belly, dip his tongue into my navel, and lick around it. With the head

93

of my cock rubbing on his cheek, he put his tongue on the side of it, licked down to my balls, and up the other side all in slow motion.

I wanted to come so bad; I tried to urge him to take me in his mouth by thrusting my hips up to bring my cock closer to where I wanted it to go. He kept licking my cock and caressing it with his lips, doing it his way, to give me the most pleasure he could, driving me mad with desire.

After what seemed an eternity, he took me all the way down his throat, and the muscles there massaged my cock as he swallowed, the feeling made me moan, and thrust my hips again as if to go deeper he gagged a bit but was controlling the reflex.

I was out of his mouth and I wanted him to take me that way again, instead, he licked down to my balls, and this time took them in his mouth and tugged on my ball sac, intense heat spread through my midsection.

He raised my legs and continued licking down between them. Up and down my thighs, back to my balls, and down between my ass cheeks. His fingers were exploring the targeted goal, teasing my sphincter by pressing gently on it.

Then his tongue found its target, he pushed his tongue in as far as it would go, the shock waves rolled over me like a tsunami. The area between my legs and ass cheeks was wet with warm saliva. His fingers were moving through the wetness, always coming back to my sphincter, and each time he touched it fresh waves of lust went through me.

I wanted it to last longer and longer, but I couldn't control it. I was going to come, and Lexi seemed to know exactly when to take me in his mouth. I shot a gallon of cum it seemed, he had me so sexually worked up, as he intended, that my release was heightened with his expert love-making.

My undamaged fingers curled around his cock, slowly stroked it a few times, rolled over, and took him in my mouth. He was as worked up as I was; he came in just a few thrusts of his cock into my mouth. Ambrosia, nectar of the gods, I ate everything he produced and kept sucking, hoping there would be more.

When we were lying in each other's arms again, Lexi said softly and lovingly, "I wanted to give you some of the pleasure you gave me today with your music and your honesty, I could never match it but I'll do it every day for you until we're even."

"You just paid off the debt, if there ever was one, with that amazingly hot sex. You know all the buttons to push and you pushed every one. I was in ecstasy; I hope I can send you there the same way you did for me."

"You do lover, every time you touch me."

A person doesn't know how it feels to be irrevocably in love until it happens to them; the euphoria makes all other encounters unimportant or forgotten. We both felt that way, we were dedicated to each other, the smallest detail became an important part of our love for each other. I was a happy man, so was Lexi.

Chapter 9

Xmas and Hydro Electric Plant

Sunday we discussed plans for the future; how to make the child, Katrina, accept being taken to NY. She was four, and if she were aware of what was happening might be further traumatized.

We agreed we would go to NY for Christmas. Mom volunteered to spend time with her in the ensuing months and gain her trust in the event we could get a Visa for her. If we couldn't get one, Katrina still had a friend to talk with and relate to. She thought it a good idea to start teaching her English too, even if we didn't take her with us.

When I figured it was not too early, I called Nana and put the call on the speakerphone so she could meet the others. She was upset when I related all that had happened and admonished me to be careful. She agreed about Katrina and said she would talk to the psychiatrists the next day, Dad relayed the criteria necessary for the Czech Medical Board decision.

Mom explained what she intended to do about Katrina until it was time to leave. Nana agreed to set up a foundation for the Electrification of Mountain River. I inquired about the children, and she assured me they were all doing well, Rilla was taking on more responsibility.

Nana had diligently searched for worthwhile causes we could fund, she wanted to give me a list of them, I convinced her it wasn't necessary, I trusted her implicitly.

She asked the obvious question, "How did you acquire a family so quickly Carl, what aren't you telling me?"

"I told you about Alexi, family and friends call him just Lexi, we're coming to NY so Lexi and I can marry, I love him and you will too Nana, his parents also, they're great." Nana was crying,

"I'm so happy for you Carl; it's about time, you deserve some happiness in your life after all you've been through. I'll be fretting over your visit until December, but if you love him, that's good enough for me, I can't wait to meet you Lexi, Mom and Dad, too."

Lexi ended the call by telling Nana, "I owe my future to you Nana, Carl has told us how you were virtually his guardian angel, I'll be eternally grateful to you for that. We're all looking forward to meeting you but I'm sure we'll talk again before December."

We ate a long leisurely lunch, spent an hour saying good-bye, and we were in the car, alone at last.

Once on the open road, Lexi said, "Come over here," I slid to the center of the seat and put my head on his shoulder, it seemed so natural to be doing things like this, when just over a week ago, I could only dream of it, and wish I could touch him. He took my hand and squeezed it gently and said, "Did I tell you yet today that I'm in love with you?"

"No you didn't and now you're going to pay for your lack of caring," I said as I place my hand on his crotch and groped his cock, he responded with an immediate hard on, I unzipped his pants and was sucking his cock in a jiffy, moaning softly he began stroking my hair,

"How did I manage without you? I love you," he cried as he spilled his seed into my eager mouth, "When we get home you'll learn what payback is like." He began groping my erection and was soon masturbating me as the car slowed.

"Step on it then I can't wait if this is your idea of revenge," he didn't miss a stroke as the car sped up. I ejaculated all over his arm and hand, he licked it off his hand, and was about to try the same on his arm when I stopped him, licked his arm clean and told him,

"I'm flattered you like the taste, but I want to get home in one piece so we can do this several more times."

Late afternoon we got back to our seldom lived in condo, Lexi made a declaration,

"We are not going to have separate bedrooms, I couldn't stand to sleep one more night away from you; I've had enough of those nights since I met you. You will sleep in my arms if I have to tie you up."

I cracked up; he was serious, but totally unnecessary,

"I have no intention of letting you sleep alone," I laughed, "It would drive me mad to have you sleeping a few feet away from me and be unable to caress your beautiful body, kiss your sweet lips, or have hot sex with you all night. If I have to I'll tie you up, I've had enough of those nights too. Let's alternate rooms every night until we agree on which is best for us."

"I'm up for that let's try your room first," he said, "Its closer."

I got the message right away, and we started undressing before we were in the bedroom. Naked, we kissed standing just inside the room and shuffled to the bed, we made love for almost 2-hours when fatigue and hunger convinced us we were sated.

We had dinner at a trendy restaurant in the university area so we wouldn't have to drive. Our first meal together, alone, in private. We toasted our good fortune, our love, and our future with a bottle of outrageously expensive Chateau Margot, Bordeaux wine. Exhausted and more than a little tipsy we happily made our way home holding hands, another fantasy became a reality.

The next week turned out to be more productive than we thought possible. Lexi suggested writing about the Mountain people, their backward living conditions, and what the government might do to change that. An offering to keep the government at bay, by suggesting economic incentives, improving utility service, and planned road construction was our strategy.

I liked his suggestion. Because of our involvement with the people, I was 'into the story', and had more interest in it than just writing an article. By noon Monday, I had a full-length feature story of the people in the Moravian area of the Carpathians. Not critical of the authorities, but very supportive of the people and the hardships they had to endure since the fall of communism.

Lexi, early Monday-morning left for the ministry of natural resources. Contrary to his expectations, everything he requested was given to him. They even made copies of the seasonal river flow report, the immaterialized plans to install generators at the falls, and the report explaining why it would not come to fruition.

Overjoyed at his good luck, he found the professor who agreed to give him the time to explain his plan and advise him of its practicality. Whatever Lexi couldn't tell him from personal observation, they pored over the reports until they found the information needed to calculate whether the project would be profitable or even feasible.

The report that caused the project to be abandoned was rife with lame excuses about the unnecessary expense in an area that had little requirement for that level of electrical power. Also the problems inherent in trying to build transmission lines across the mountains. According to the report, the cost to benefit ratio had the benefit side as the big loser.

The professor sadly shook his head, "This was written shortly after the fall of communism, the new regime only knew how short of money they were, not what benefits would accrue from a long-term project. It's not that they didn't want to help, it simply couldn't be justified when the whole of Czechoslovakia was literally falling apart."

He added "Now it's a different story, there are chronic power shortages with demand growing daily. I'm thinking of a strategy that would achieve your goals, and not be so prohibitively expensive."

"First, according to the seasonal flow chart, there are millions of gallons of water going over those falls every minute of the day winter and summer. Second, your quick calculation on output was off by a few million kilowatts. Lastly, if the cavern behind the falls is as big as you think it is—they apparently didn't know it even existed, it would cut the costs by a third; it's expensive to build with water running over you."

"You told me you think there's another way in where would that be located?"

"Approximately a mile up the river from the town, on the opposite side above the falls, there may be access from farther up the river we were too wet and cold to even try to find out, but it's on our list. A map was with the material I got and shows a road about a half-mile above the falls, if it's an existing road there would be a bridge, but the map doesn't indicate one way or the other."

The professor went to his computer and pulled up a Czech road map for the Carpathian Mountains.

"Sure enough there's a bridge, but how old? And in what state of repair? I guess you have something else to check on. The bridge would have to hold 50-tons or more, turbines and generators are heavy."

"They may be able to reinforce it that would be cheaper than building a new bridge, the roads have to take that kind of weight too, or they could collapse into the river, they're very close. All this is fixable, not cheap, and not easy, but less than not having existing roads."

"We were thinking of approaching the government to propose a private/public partnership. In the agreement the government would improve the roads through the mountains, build a high-tension modern transmission system, to Hodonin, upgrade the line coming in from Olomouc, and now reinforce the bridge or maybe build a new one."

"Our Electrification Foundation will purchase and install the turbines and generators, build the control systems, and bring the operation online. The generating station will be run by a private management company with government oversight."

"Operating jointly, will be a local economic development fund, any profits realized after the costs of line maintenance, management contract and repairs, will be used to fund it. The Electrification Foundation is nonprofit. An exploratory group will be set up at our expense before we approach the government."

"Someone gave this a lot of thought, who is going to head this exploratory group?"

"We were hoping it would be you. Are you interested?"

"I'm very interested, what's your time frame? I have until September if that will work."

"It shouldn't take any longer than that. Would you be willing to sit and negotiate with the Bureaucracy after we have our findings?"

The professor smiled and said, "With relish."

Lexi was beside himself with excitement when he got back. "Carl this is going to work, the professor is on our side he has impressive credentials. He even agreed to be part of our legation to the government. He would like to view the site this weekend if that's not a problem."

"My lover is a silver-tongued devil; can anyone resist your charm? That's the best news we could get. If we're going back this weekend, we had better start planning what we're going to need to explore that cavern; did you talk about that with him?"

"Yes, he said he knows just the right people to take with him, it seems he still has many contacts in the industry. I told him there may be some trouble with local thugs, he suggested we bring along a few security guards who can handle assholes."

"He didn't say assholes."

"He did, I might have called them assholes earlier, but he did say it."

"Well, call a spade a spade I guess. Do you think Mom or Dad would know where we could hire a half-dozen reliable security guards?"

"Let's call and find out," he said as he picked up the phone,

Mom answered, Lexi told her we were going back to the waterfall's cavern, and asked her if she knew any security people,

"We employ a security firm at the hospital; do you want me to ask them if they have 6-guards you could rent for the weekend? Do you want them armed?"

"Not necessarily, if they are legally carrying it's all right with us. Mom, one other thing could you reserve a van for us, an 8-passenger, for Saturday morning?"

"I'll call you back as soon as I have something."

Lexi and I started a list of the hardware we would need going into the cave again. This gear would be carried up the path for a mile; we tried to keep it to necessities so we could respond to an emergency. We added and subtracted for an hour, when Mom called back we took a break for lunch and discussed our plans with her. She had arranged for guards on Saturday at 9:00 a.m., and the van delivered to the house at 8:00 a.m.

Mom was amazed we had moved so fast and jokingly added "After what I encountered in that motel room I shouldn't be surprised, you two don't waste a minute." We laughed at Moms ribald comment and told her to expect us on Friday.

Another hour was spent on our list and we compromised on many items. Our predominant requirement was light, but many kinds of lights are available. We settled on lightweight halogens we found on the Internet.

Attachable to helmets, and waterproof, they gave off bright light requiring minimal battery power that fit in a vest pocket. They were perfect for venturing into the cavern. We added two powerful lantern type gas lamps to give some bright light to gauge the size of the cavern.

Next in importance was slickers with pull-up hoods, waterproof footwear, weather proof carrying sacks for cameras, a small transit, a good quality recorder, measuring tools, and rope. Eight men could easily carry that much equipment without laboring, and could easily discard it in the event of an emergency.

Still only midafternoon, it made sense to get as much shopping out of the way as possible. The specialty store that sold the helmet mounted lights was in reality a sporting goods store, but it had some really neat devices, such as video cameras worn on a chain around the neck or on a lapel.

Hidden, battery operated camera kits were purchased that unless you were familiar with this style of snooping you'd never pick it out. They also carried slickers and boots it was one stop shopping, or almost anyway.

Wednesday, we called Nana, she informed us there was now an, 'Electrification for River Town Foundation' with a $200,000 account transferred to our bank in Prague, International banking is so easy.

We continued picking up small items for our excursion and by Thursday we had all our equipment purchased; the condo was overflowing it seemed with gear for exploring. To transport all that equipment we needed an SUV, for the family we were hoping to become.

Lexi, as usual, was nervous about buying a car; he wanted to adhere to our original budget, using only the money we earned. I convinced him that renting a car and paying for gas and mileage would be the same as making a monthly payment.

The SUV would be in his name, I wasn't a permanent resident or citizen, so I wasn't allowed to own a car, drive one, yes, rent one, yes, buy one, no.

Making the rounds of car lots, Lexi spotted a new Audi SUV, and there was no talking him out of it.

"It's not really a foreign car; this one was made next door in Slovakia." He claimed, we had agreed on a used car, "We won't be buying someone's trouble, it will have a full warrantee, and we'll know where it's been and how it's used."

I gave up trying. We bought a pearl white beauty, big, and not a mommy wagon for picking up the kiddies at school. I liked it too; I just wanted to win a point about spending money. We became the owners of a new Audi SUV, nice vehicle. Friday we packed the gear into the SUV and headed to Brno.

Like most new-car owners Lexi was adamant about the cleanliness of his 'ride', no eating in the car; was the first edict, and sheets to cover seats where we placed new equipment.

When we were on the road, I almost regretted getting the car. I had scooted over to be close, ready to perform some not so magic tricks, when I put my hand on his leg he was horrified,

"Carl, we're going to get stuff all over the seat."

It struck me as hilarious, I laughed so hard tears were running down my face. When I turned to look at him he had a sheepish grin on his face,

"I guess that's over the top," he smirked, "Come here we'll make one exception to the rule, you can do that anytime you want."

I did. He thawed quickly about keeping the car in pristine condition, mostly because he wanted sex more than he cared about cleaning up a little mess off the seats; they were leather for God's sake.

We stopped at the car rental agency, signed the rental agreement, and gave them my credit card. Mom had already arranged for the time and place of delivery, so we continued to Mom and Dad's house.

Mom was full of anxiety, she had been thinking about our request for information on the availability of security guards,

"I've been wondering how wise this little expedition is, you have no idea what you're up against, what if there's a mob of them, enough to overpower you?"

"Mom no one knows we're going up there, to get a mob together the villagers would notice the village being emptied of assholes, and know who was responsible for any trouble that arises, if that doesn't work you can call in the army." Lexi responded.

"You always have a rational explanation but bad things happen, and I fear my boys getting hurt."

"We'll be careful, there's ways to do this so it's unexpected, and therefore little time to mount a well-planned assault on us" Lexi assured her.

"Come have lunch with me, your father is speaking with some members of the Medical Board about Katrina, he'll be along shortly."

Dad joined us 10-minutes later and related what he had learned from the Medical Board,

"Katrina's initial prognosis is not good, she's become autistic, but it's unclear whether this was caused by the trauma she endured, or whether it's an existing condition. If it were preexisting, there is no chance they will determine it to be a medical emergency."

"When you get there tomorrow ask Tomas casually if he knew what the child was like, I'm sure everyone knows everyone else in a village that small; if she were autistic Tomas would know something was wrong with her. That will put a new light on their review."

"Let's assume the autism is trauma induced, it will require many hours of therapy most likely utterly ineffective, little is known about autism, its cure, at any rate, if we have a psychiatric team of specialists in childhood trauma it's a good bet they will agree to an exit visa. The ball is back in your court."

"Is there telephone service in the village?" Mom asked,

"When Carl jumped in the river, I gave Tomas my cell phone to call you, the only phone in the village is in the constable's office. Tomas isn't sure he's not one of the bullies so we're cutting him out of any involvement in our investigation."

Lexi's answer gave me an idea, "How about giving Tomas a cell phone? We could stay in contact after we leave the village to go to the cavern and he can watch to see if anyone is following us. You and Dad will at least have a way to check on us if we haven't gotten in touch in a reasonable time."

"Last week we bought video cameras to monitor reaction to our activities, maybe we should focus one on the footbridge considering it's the only way to the falls except from above them," Lexi added, "We could train one on the constable's office also, it might be interesting to see who visits him after we leave the village."

We finished lunch and Dad drove us to a little store that sold security devices and spy gear. We found a device with a beam that when broken sends a signal to a receiver, then resets.

It would, in effect, tell us whether there was more than one follower. Lexi noted they might come into the ravine from the pastureland above, so we got two, operating on different wavelengths, we'd each carry a receiver, and be able to outflank any attackers.

On the way home we discussed strategy for approaching the village. Two vehicles carrying several men each, pulling into the village at the same time wouldn't be smart. Our arrival times had to be staggered to mitigate panic at what might be perceived as an invasion. Lexi, our inveterate strategist, suggested,

"We go past the village," he said, as if in deep concentration, "Find the bridge; check it for safety then go down the river on the other side to see if we can locate the other entrance."

"If we can't find it, we reconnoiter the area that the fork of the path leads to and see whether some of us can reach the falls from that direction, that way if we are being watched in the village, the watchers won't know our strength."

"We'll call the Professor when we know if the cave is accessible from the other side or not. We could send five of the security guards down to the lower path while we go to the inn to meet the Professor with only one security guard."

Dad was beaming at him, "You have this all thought out with precision; the military could use that brain of yours. You still have two vehicles going to the village; you'd have to leave some time between arrivals."

"Right, I figured it would take 15 to 20-minutes for the guards to get down to the fork, they could even wait up above for a few minutes for us to get down to the village, then proceed on down and wait for us at the forks, set the infrared devices and check them out while they're waiting."

"Now you know why I wanted to be partners with this guy, he's brilliant, as well as having many other attributes," I said, with a look promising him tonight will be momentous.

Dad gave us a knowing look and nodded in agreement.

CHAPTER 10

STRATEGY TO THWART AN AMBUSH

Back home we spread the maps on the kitchen table, and spent almost an hour calculating the distance from the village to the bridge. Then from the bridge back down to the falls, the falls appeared to be halfway between the village and the bridge.

We calculated again, from the highway side of the bridge to where the path descended to the river and from the village to the fork in the path. Our goal was to get some idea how long we could take checking on the other side of the bridge for a second entrance.

The map wasn't all that accurate, the distances indicated by the map weren't as great as shown, which gave us more time, thankfully. We eventually decided that if we left Brno at 9-o'clock and the professor left Prague at 9-o'clock we would be 2-hours ahead of him. We would have plenty of time to survey the area south of the river, and reconnoiter the pasture land north of the river leading to the fork in the lower path.

When we were ready to execute the plan, we would contact the Professor to note his location, and calculate the time it would take for each vehicle to reach the inn, and create a 10-minute difference in arrivals. Confident we had every eventuality covered; we packed up our map and new purchases, then took Mom and Dad out to dinner.

I made good my implied promise made earlier in the car. We took a shower together, I washed his hot body, every square inch of him was lovingly scrubbed and caressed. He responded in kind, and two very sexually aroused lovers left the shower, toweled dry, and bounded onto the bed.

With his legs dangling over the side of the bed, I ran my tongue up the inside of his thighs. I licked, and sucked his balls, took the head of his cock in my mouth and circled his glans where the foreskin was attached. With my tongue I moved his foreskin over the head, kept my tongue inside the foreskin licking around and around the head,

Lexi was moaning and thrusting his hips up for more pleasure. My fingers were stroking his anus, and his groin was spasming with involuntary muscle contractions from my tongue and fingers actions. Meanwhile, my other hand caressed his smooth, round, ass cheeks.

The effect on me, rubbing my cock against his leg was bringing me close to coming, and I wanted this to last. I loved sucking his cock, but he wanted to suck mine too, his hand kept reaching down in search of it. I turned around, and he greedily swallowed me as I swallowed him, we impaled each other with our cocks, and loved it. Seconds later we were shooting hot sperm into each other's mouth.

I pulled him up on the bed, and we kissed for 10-minutes, he rolled onto his back, lifted one leg, took my cock, and rubbed it on his exposed sphincter. I wanted to rim him in the worst way, but he was already inviting me in, and my cock, hot, and horny, pushed its way into paradise.

This position was better than legs over shoulders, our bodies were in contact in many more places, and I could masturbate him while I was all the way inside him rocking back and forth, my hand on his cock moving up and down. It feels like no other sensation there is, and we slowed down to make it last, we had all night after all.

It worked to a small degree, just a few minutes of ecstasy later, we were releasing a flood of semen, his, on his chest and belly, mine, deep inside him. After cleaning up he lay in my arms, his head on my chest and asked me,

"Carl I love you fucking me, it feels wonderful, but does it make me the female? Will I end up being exactly what I hate?"

"Male and female don't exist in our relationship, you are as much a man as I am, maybe more, who cares? If you want to fuck me, just say the word or better still, rip my clothes off, and do the caveman routine, don't ask permission, fuck me like a whore in a cheap motel–just kiss me when you're finished. Don't worry about becoming a nellie queen, you're way too masculine to carry it off, they'd throw you out of the club."

Assured that we were still two males making love, not playing roles, we fell asleep, refreshing, and dreamless until 7:00. Ten minutes later, Mom was urging a breakfast large enough for 4-people on us, "You may not eat again for hours, and you're going to need fuel to keep up your energy, now eat."

Lexi muttered "Like we have a choice."

"I heard that Lexi, excuse me for looking out for you." Mom complained.

"Did you get up on the wrong side of the bed? Or are you worried about what we're doing?" Lexi said, "You think I believe you don't care? Mom you know better than that. This has nothing to do with food."

"I'm scared Lexi, it's my job as a mother to worry about her two beautiful sons who may or may not come back," she tried to hide her tears unsuccessfully.

"Don't worry, we'll call you every chance we get to keep you up on how it's going, I mean four or five times today, okay?"

"I won't worry, but I'll sit by the phone all day," she grudgingly conceded.

The telephone rang, and broke the tension, we giggled nervously. The head of our security guards called to say they were on their way, and would be here in fewer than 30-minutes. The van showed up 5-minutes later, as if it were a good omen. We went out the front door, and Mom saw the Audi for the first time.

"When did you get that?" she asked, "That's not a rental."

Answering before Lexi could say anything, I said, "Lexi bought it yesterday, he fell in love with it, and twisted my arm until I cried uncle."

Lexi was sputtering, "You agreed, I didn't buy it myself."

I gave him a hug, and said to Mom, "I'm kidding, we love it, and it's so pretty we don't want to get it dirty." Lexi gave me a punch on the arm, but was smiling.

We emptied the Audi, and separated the items so we could distribute them to the security guards. We put six waterproof slickers, helmets, and boots aside for the Professor and his crew; we would distribute the other items when we got to the bridge. It wasn't even 8:30 when the security detail showed up.

Mom made a big pot of coffee; we sat around the kitchen table while Lexi explained our plans. Few questions were asked. All were 'carrying', and all legally. The leader of the group said he knew the roads up there from many hunting excursions, he volunteered to drive.

Lexi gave no argument; he was in fact, relieved. We kissed Mom good-bye, and started down the drive at a minute or two before 9:00. On the road Lexi called the Professor to synchronize our watches, and relate any last-minute information.

By the time the Professor was arriving in Brno; we planned to be on the bridge, it would give us about an hour and a half to play detective. Our driver was good, but cautious, and it was closer to 2-hours to make it to the falls.

A call to the Professor gave an idea of our time constraints, he was just leaving Brno, we told him to take his time and drive carefully, we'd call again in 2-hours.

We found the bridge and everyone got out of the van. We were less than 2-miles past the village, much closer to the falls than the map indicated. The bridge was also closer to the road than we had calculated, about one kilometer, a half-mile. Not a house or farm was in sight the area was desolate.

Lexi called Mom as he had promised and told her we were checking out the bridge, we would call later. We walked across the bridge to check as best we could the stability and strength of the structure. It appeared to have recent traffic pass over it, and no discernable rust was on the girders, the roadbed was blacktop and in good condition, we decided to drive across it.

The guard's intrepid leader, Loic, walked back to the van, and drove across the bridge, it didn't move or even shake. I stood on the bridge to see if there would be any ominous noises, nothing, the structure was strong enough to bear the weight of the van.

Only 50-feet of road continued on the other side going straight ahead to a rock wall towering 40-feet above the road. An outcropping of rock, 200-feet wide, jutted from the mountain-side on a steep slant for about 500-feet, probably the support base for that end of the bridge.

The road ran both ways from the short approach to the bridge; the falls would be to the left. Driving down the dirt road a short distance we spotted the falls on the left side, again much closer to the bridge than the map indicated. The area had widened after passing the rock outcropping, still no structures, just grassy pasture land.

Farther down, the road took a sharp turn to the right, and continued between two outcroppings, then disappeared as it turned left through a pass. We disembarked the vehicle again, the side of the road along the river was covered with boulders, and brush, laurel, and alder covered the ground almost completely. This was disappointing, if there's another entrance we would most likely have to find it from inside the cavern.

Still, we strolled down the road toward the falls. A short distance past where we had stopped, a guard noticed an opening in the laurel that would accommodate one man if he stooped and turned sideways. Deer are about the only creatures that can navigate in a laurel grove, so this had to have been hacked out by a human.

Single file, Lexi, two of the guards, and I squeeze through the narrow opening, 4 or 5-feet in, it widened to about 4-feet and wound around the densest parts of the underbrush. Forty-feet from the road the trail led to a large pile of rocks, and the trail ended.

Brush on both sides, and a large pile of rocks in front of us, made no sense. Lexi solved the mystery, 6-feet out from the rocks, debris from wind, and winter storms, branches, and leaves, was piled a foot or more deep.

He started kicking the stuff out of the way as if he were about to climb the rock pile, when we heard a distinct knock from his shoe hitting a piece of wood. Excitedly we swept the area clean of debris, and found a wooden door in the ground.

A set of stairs beneath the door was hidden by the rock pile artfully placed to give headroom, but it appeared to be randomly piled stones.

Lexi, ever eager for adventure made a move to go down the steps, I jumped to stop him, but a security guard pulled him back first.

"I just want to go to the bottom of the steps to see if it's the cavern," he said.

"You don't have a light, we can't see the bottom of the steps, the only way you're going down there is with the rest of us," I told him forcefully, "So let's go back to the van, discuss what we found, and make an intelligent decision on how to proceed."

The guard nodded in agreement, though he was not well versed in English, he understood my reluctance to venture into that dark hole with no lights for any reason.

We left the crude door open, and returned to the road. The four guards were nervously pacing around the van, there had been no traffic, but they all claimed that someone was watching. They probably had infected each other with that idea based solely on a feeling.

I had an idea, which I knew would appeal to Lexi, "Let's call the Professor and tell him to come here instead of the inn, we can all go in this way without all the village knowing we're here, or planning to go in the cave."

"We have to go to the inn," Lexi replied, "We need for Tomas to have the cell phone to warn us. I'm sure they already know we're here, we drove through the village, a dozen people must have seen us."

"Don't discredit the guards' feeling of being watched, if someone got the idea we were headed here, it would be easy to send a watcher across the footbridge, and up this side of the river. They could have been here while we were inspecting the bridge."

"You're right as usual, so if they already know, there may be goons headed for the waterfall entrance now, a warning from Tomas would come too late, and we'll be ambushed going in either way." I replied, "I think the only way we're going to get in there is to go in both ways at once and create a diversion, on this side it would be easier."

The chief suggested throwing a lighted flare into the cavern, several were in the van for emergencies on the road.

"That would be a surprise for sure if they think we don't know they're going to ambush us," I could see Lexi's mind turning over possibilities, "Maybe more than one, a couple from each side would really throw them off guard." He said.

"There's one other thing, we have to go to the inn if we're going to in under the falls, or see if there's a way down to the path from the bridge.

That's only a few minutes walk, let's take a couple of the guards, and see what options we have."

We had arrived at the bridge 45-minutes before, we still had time to check out the other side quickly and get back in time to take whatever action was required. We knew that a path went up to the elevation of the bridge, but not that it went all the way in that direction. The chief insisted he drive us back to the bridge to save time.

Once across the bridge, we found a path running down a short incline from the road to some trees on the side of a pasture. We hadn't noticed it on the way in because of the trees, but on the ground at the bottom of the incline, we could see the path stretching down the side of the river for quite a distance before our view was blocked by the trees.

Rather than going down a continuation of the path that undoubtedly forked up the side of the ravine, we headed back to the others. We still had 45-minutes to develop a strategy to thwart an attack before the Professor arrived.

Lexi suggested we get Tomas and some men he trusted to visit the constable with us that would take him out of the action if he's one of the thugs. The river and paths were communal property; he wouldn't be able to justify forbidding us to check out the falls with a group of villagers who would benefit from the electrification project.

Lexi was exactly the person to convince them, by making them come to the conclusion he wanted.

We decided the professor would not stop in the village, but come directly here. Lexi and I, and two guards would go to the village; we unloaded all our gear except what the four of us required, who would make the assault from under the falls.

We set our cell phones for speed dialing, and placed one of the infrared monitors on the entrance through the laurels in the event anyone came out of the cave to take the four guards by surprise.

The four positioned themselves to see in every direction, but principally to see the bridge and the path up the side of the river, the road between the outcroppings was in the open, so anyone approaching from there would be seen immediately.

"If a vehicle comes across the bridge, hunker down behind the huge rocks scattered about. If you have trouble, fire a warning shot, and make them dive for cover, call us the minute you're able to."

"When the Professor arrives, you'll leave two guards with the vehicle, the rest will cautiously approach the cave's back door. Don't go in until we call your cell phone, the noise of the falls, as you can tell from here, is deafening. Put your phones on vibrate, if we call once it means holdback, if it vibrates, stops, and vibrates again means we're going in, and you should do the same."

"Make sure the stairs and passage to the cavern are clear. Proceed with the utmost caution to as close to the cavern as safely dictates, so the flares can be thrown as far into the cave as possible, one as far left as you can, and the other straight ahead. The water is to your right, and there's some light, so they probably won't be there."

"We'll come in from the ledge behind the falls up to the blind wall. When your first flare fires up, we'll throw one to the right, and one to the center that should make enough light to read by. We turn our helmet lights on simultaneously, and sweep the cave for hiding places."

We went over it once more and we left for the village our gear hidden from view. We called the Professor and filled him in on our plans. We mentioned our concern that the constable would try to stop us from checking out the falls,

"I know how territorial some of these small town constables can be, I went to the Ministry of the Interior who has jurisdiction over them, and got written permission to investigate the possibility of a hydroelectric generating station on that river in that waterfall. All signed sealed and stamped," he pronounced, "It's his job if he refuses us."

117

One more hurdle out of the way, but if the constable's in cahoots with the bad guys he could still cause us much trouble. Tomas was happy to see us until Lexi told him of our plans; he wore a worried look and said.

"Earlier this morning one bully I told you about was walking very fast up to the footbridge; he was almost running by the time he got across the bridge. It looked strange, but he's a strange guy."

"Suspicions confirmed," Lexi remarked, "Does anyone in the village have a cell phone that you know of?"

"No one here can afford such a luxury, I never even saw one until you let me use yours, someone in the village would see such a thing and everyone would know, that's what happened when I used yours."

Lexi asked him to get a couple of good men who he trusted to go to the constable with us. He frowned but agreed, he asked a boy to fetch back two men, and the boy scampered out, he was back in 5-minutes with 2-men Lexi had spoken with before.

They greeted us warmly, and Lexi started explaining the plan to bring enough electricity to service all the towns up here with much excess power to sell to Hodonin or Olomouc. Any money made from the sale of excess electricity will stimulate economic growth right here.

They bought it, he explained we had to see the constable, to make sure it was all right, and they loudly objected,

"He is not our ruler he is a peacekeeper the people decide things like this."

Lexi you are a wonder, you would be a very successful con artist if you were wired that way, thank God you're on our side.

The constable was not a bit surprised to see us; it almost seemed as if he were expecting us. Lexi started by telling him that we had a team of engineers to check out the falls for hydroelectric.

"You're wasting your time," he said, "The government already did that and turned it down. I don't want you getting people all excited for nothing."

Tomas stepped in, "That was more than 30-years ago, things are much different now, and the people of this village will welcome a study for this proposal, you have no authority to stop them."

"If I consider it disturbing the peace I can," he boasted, "I'll run them out of my district if I have a mind to"

"How will you explain that to the Ministry of the Interior?" Lexi calmly asked, "They gave us written permission to conduct this study. How badly do you want to keep your job?"

The constable turned lipstick red and looked about to explode, "Who do you think you are, coming here and telling me what I can or can't do, and threatening my job?"

Lexi as cool as ever replied, "No one is threatening your job, I'm telling you if you don't comply with the Ministry's written orders they will replace you for impeding progress."

"This is an expensive study, if we are forced to postpone it after bringing our experts all this way, someone is going to pay, if you are the cause of the postponement, you will pay, with your job."

The blood drained from his face, he was still defiant, and it made me wonder whether he answered to an authority more powerful, and feared more than the Ministry he worked for.

"Show me this permission," he snarled, "Or you can go to hell."

"The head of our exploratory group has it," Lexi smiled and said, "I'll call him and have him stop here on the way to the falls."

We turned and walked out of his office. Lexi called immediately as we left, "Professor where are you now?"

"Just approaching the bridge," he replied.

"Turn around and come to the village there's been a change for the better."

Before he could disappear, the Professor's car pulled up in front of the constable. Confronted by an edict from the Ministry, and the delegation of villagers, he was cowed and impotent in his rage. I thought

119

that if his employer orders him to do his job, and the people he is sworn to protect don't persuade him to capitulate, what would, abject humiliation?

The Professor could be imperious when his authority was challenged, and the constable was challenging him. He was like old-time royalty when no one had the temerity to talk back to the King. He gave the constable the abject humiliation he deserved.

The Professor demanded the constable accompany us to the falls, this was heavier than a Wagnerian Opera. We left for the falls, the constable following, docile as a lamb.

The guards were confused when we drove up to where they were waiting, we quickly explained, and the objection to our new plan was voiced as quickly,

"Constable or not we are still going to be ambushed going in on one side only," the chief deduced, "Why can't we go in both ways, it's not that far to the other side, we could be in place in 10 or 15-minutes, I'll take three of my men and Lexi, and we'll do it the way we planned."

Lexi, of course, agreed and changed it a bit, "I don't think we need five to handle that side. I'll go because I know where we're going, two more to handle any unexpected rear action and the flares, it's a pretty tight area not really enough room for five."

My heart was in my throat, please be careful, I silently pleaded.

"Okay, check if we have everything we need, matches, one infrared sensor, cell phone, flares, and our rain gear, let's go." The three jumped in the van and were off, heading back to the bridge.

I was the skunk at the wedding, everyone was talking and I understood nothing they discussed, the professor saw my dilemma and explained what was going on, they were trying to decide what to do with the constable.

"Make him go in first," I said, "If he refuses too strenuously we'll know it's an ambush."

"Excellent idea I'll try that."

He quickly told the others we were going in, leaving two guards to watch the vehicles, motioning us to start, he stayed beside the constable, they were second and third in line.

We went through the narrow opening and proceeded to the hidden door. Helmet lights came on to view the bottom area of the stairway, no traps, or people hiding.

A tunnel led away from the stairs at a downward slope. I figured the stairs to go 12-feet below the surface; we still had to drop more than 80-feet to reach the floor of the cavern. We weren't that far from the river, to comfortably navigate the incline there must be multiple switchbacks on the way down.

Light was coming in from overhead as we made a sharp left turn on the inclined floor, the tunnel had ended at the turn and, now we were in a gallery of sorts ramping downward with openings every 10-feet to a vast area indiscernible because of the darkness.

The professor was holding the constables arm as he propelled him down the ramp. The constable didn't appear worried about an ambush; he seemed in a trance, stumbling every few feet, head drooping then bobbing up again, shuffling rather than walking; he was like a condemned man going to the gallows.

We stopped, and decided the other three should be in place, we lit our flares. They blossomed into huge circles of light in the darkness, falling toward a floor still 40-feet below. Two more flares blossomed on the opposite side of the cavern, and with all four burning brightly we could see a group of 5-men shielding their eyes from the bright light, and making angry noises.

The Professor yelled, "Constable, arrest those men."

The group suddenly fell silent, Lexi and the two guards came around the blind wall, and with all lights on, the two lanterns, and the four flares we got a good all-around view of the cavern. The arched, vaulted ceiling was possibly 70-feet-high, the sides 80 to 90-feet wide and from the water curtain to the rear, indiscernible.

Our group began running down the incline and suddenly came to stairs that switched back several times in their journey to the floor; no one fell, but piled up as those of us in front stopped to get our bearings. The stairs helped us get to the bottom faster than a ramp, we fanned out in front of the group of attackers, Loic already had his weapon trained on them.

They were ignoring us and staring at the constable,

"Ivor, what are you doing here?" one asked, baffled that the constable was with those they were supposed to attack, "The Master told you to stay in the village."

Recovering somewhat, the constable shouted,

"Shut up you fool."

The security chief challenged the constable, "Who and where is the Master? You are one of them," he screamed in his face, "I'll see you behind bars for this, and the Ministry will have a few charges of their own."

The constable and five thugs said nothing; they looked morose, and guilty as hell. The guards disarmed the thugs, tied them securely with arms behind their backs, and marched them out of the cave.

CHAPTER 11

A HAUNTED CAVERN

Outside the cavern he put in a call to the National Police, and related the events of the morning. When they learned the Professor and his study group were commissioned by the Ministry of the Interior it became a Federal matter, they would take over the case, and the prisoners.

A police helicopter was dispatched from Olomouc and would be at the falls in 2-hours. The constable was not directly involved and would be subject to local police jurisdiction, whatever that was.

With the threat of ambush removed, the Professor and his experts went to work. They brought large banks of sodium lights with them, and in very short time the inside of the cavern was bright as day. The experts were measuring and checking the bottom of the falls from inside the cavern. Lexi and I were left alone, squeezing his hand, I told him I was scared shitless for him while he was gone, he squeezed back, and said he was too, my brave teddy bear.

We snooped around the cave checking every little niche, until we came to the stairs to the back entrance as we called it. Behind the stairs were more stairs going down. The Professor came to check out our find with two of his associates. This development intrigued them, previously they were trying to determine why the stairs had been carved into the rock and by whom.

The only indisputable fact so far was that the cavern was very old and may have been some religious cult's secret sanctuary. The Professor speculated that there may be a series of caverns beneath the floor, and a determination had to be made whether the floor of this upper cavern would support the heavy generators.

One of the group had gone for a large light, when he came back we started down the stairs. The chamber at the bottom of the stairs was from a horror movie; in the middle of this space sat an altar, covered with a dark-brown substance that could only be dried blood. All around the room Iron rings were fastened into the rock walls interspersed with holders for torches.

The room was repulsive; we decided to have a survey team map the chambers that opened off this one, and an engineer to determine the strength of the floor.

We went back to the main cavern, and while waiting for the Professor to finish we tried to sort the bizarre things we had heard and seen. We started with the constable's demeanor in his office that seemed he was beholden to a different power from the Interior Ministry.

I told Lexi how the constable was acting on the way down to the floor of the cavern I believe he was thoroughly terrorized, and he only snapped out of it when one of the goons called him Ivor, I presume that's his name, and mentioned the Master.

"My bet is that this master is the one he's so terrified of," I said, "If he fails the master he dies, probably as the tourists did, no blood in the bodies but plenty on that altar, a connection you think?"

Lexi deep in thought nodded his head, "I think we've stumbled onto something Carl, the locals are petrified when this place is mentioned. You saw Tomas' reaction when we told him we were here; he said this place is evil. I'll bet it's been 'evil' for literally centuries. The villagers are afraid to answer questions for fear of some master. That is our next mystery to solve. What is this place really?"

"I don't know, but I'm starting to feel woozy, I think there may be some gas seepage in here, it occurs in certain caves."

"I don't feel so perky myself, but I thought it was because of what we saw down below," Lexi agreed, "A geologist might be able to confirm that. Let's have it checked out, it could be hallucinogenic. That would explain the torture and human sacrifices, the rings on the walls weren't for tying up animals."

"If there is seepage of a hallucinogenic gas Lexi, how can we have a control room here for the generating station?"

"If a gas is present, the geologist will be able to tell us how to seal it off. We should wait until the place is surveyed, and we know what we're dealing with. I'm going to ask the Professor if he or any of his crew feel light headed as we do."

As Lexi sought out the Professor, I wrote notes as I have been doing practically all my life, it's a lot better reminder than a string around the finger. As I wrote, it occurred to me that the body of the stabbed husband might be down here somewhere, if the drag marks were made by feet, something was brought in here that doesn't naturally belong here. We should look for it.

My plans for a search were overridden by Lexi. After finding the Professor felt light headed, as we did, he inquired of the others and four out of five said they did feel as I had put it 'woozy'.

"We're getting out of here," Lexi pronounced, "We have no idea what we're inhaling, I don't think it's deadly, there's been people in here with no apparent long-lasting effects, but it could intoxicate us for who knows how long. We have a long ride back to Brno and the Professor to Prague."

The Professor had finished the preliminary investigation, the questions of floor strength and gas seepage had to be answered before he could go on.

"The cavern is large enough for the number of generators these falls can handle if the floor is strong enough. It's not a clear span room below, there are plenty of support walls, and the floor is at least 12-foot thick, my professional assessment is that we're okay."

"We don't know if beneath the lower rooms it's a honeycomb that will collapse when several hundred tons are placed on the main floor, a sonic graph would clear up any questions in that regard. The base of the falls is also stable bedrock there is plenty of room for several large turbines."

"The gas seepage is another thing; gas from deep in the Earth rises into caves like these and permeates any porous rock it touches. When the level of gas recedes from the cave, the rocks slowly release their gas, it's called out-gassing. In a closed environment like here it would take some time to free the place of any residual gas, assuming the place can be sealed."

"Will you handle the geology investigation? Carl and I want to do the gas part; we think it may have something to do with what's been happening here for centuries." Lexi explained, "We can use the same geologist probably, but we want a toxicologist and a chemist to investigate the gas also, so we know if it's hallucinogenic with long exposure to it."

"You boys make me proud to be part of this project; most people would throw up their hands and leave after what we experienced today," he stated, "Which may have happened 30-years ago, that would make sense, it scared the bejesus out of them, so they made up all those lame excuses to scuttle the project."

"I know just the person to do the geologist report, he does a lot of work on Radon gas contamination, and he'll know a way to seal this place correctly."

"Our number-one priority is to get this place surveyed and sonically probed to discover what's here, I said, we're wasting our time if that report is negative."

"I'll take care of that, and schedule it for as soon as possible, I'll let you know on Monday when the survey will be done, I'm asking for a map of all caverns connected to these also. I take it you want to be here?"

"Absolutely," Lexi exclaimed, "I wouldn't miss it for anything. This is our first project together, and we're going to make it work."

The first project, which means there'll be a second, he's going to work with me, with his determination; the two of us can change the world. I'm convinced my luck has changed, and it's all because I met Lexi.

While we waited for the Federal Police helicopter, we helped the Professor stow his gear and said good-bye until next week. Loic had the goons trussed like thanksgiving turkeys, taking no chance they would run.

The constable was standing nearby, realizing he had nowhere to go and no one to give him shelter. He was resigned to his fate, he failed his Master, and his employer, he would face the employer rather than face a certain death from his evil Master if he stayed on here.

I asked the chief what we could do with him, he replied, "I'm going to get the Federals to turn him over to the Moravia District authorities, they will decide what to charge him with."

The sound of the helicopter reached us over the roar of the falls, and a large Huey helicopter appeared over the trees. They had located the village, then followed the river to the falls, they were low so it was easy to see us. The pilot set it down in the pasture and put the rotors in free spin. Three Federal Police Officers disembarked, ducked under the rotors, and headed across the road.

We gave them our signed statements; the chief had been in law enforcement and knew the procedures. They took the goons into custody, shepherded them to the helicopter, reluctantly allowing the constable to board, climbed aboard also, and took off.

I took Lexi and the chief up the road a way so we could talk over the roar of the falls, then asked,

"Do you think the government will sweep this under the rug like the two bodies they took away? I think a call to the news media that the Federal Police are on their way to Olomouc with the constable of a mountain village and 5-would-be-assassins in custody. A short explanation would bring attention to the villager's predicament, and force the government to investigate what's going on here."

They agreed. The chief called the TV news in Olomouc, identified himself to give creditability to his tip-off adding that he was enraged at almost being killed, and didn't want the authorities covering it up. For better or worse, the cat was out of the bag.

I wondered how much of what had happened had found its way back to the village and how would the villagers accept the arrest of their constable and five of the village denizens. A mile from the village we could see a mob of people on the side of the main road, to say we were nervous is an understatement.

We pulled off the main road in front of the constable's office, Tomas was standing in the doorway, he raised his arm and pandemonium broke out, it was not an angry crowd as we first believed, they congratulated us on getting rid of the constable, The village had tried for years to end his bullying and arrogance, but he managed to hold his job, Tomas told us later,

"You have done us a great service, not only ridding us of that petty tyrant, but also five of the worst troublemakers in the village. It will once again be a peaceful and serene place to live."

"You know we caught them about to ambush us in the cavern don't you?" Lexi asked.

"The whole village knows what happened," Tomas answered, "We are praying you will rid us of the evil that resides there. Will you clean them all out, so we don't have to live in fear?"

The opening Lexi had waited for, presented itself, "We are going to do everything you want us to do. We are going ahead with the electrical generating station, we have to check a few details, but so far it looks good."

"Tell me what you mean by, clean them all out?" Lexi asked, looking Tomas in the eye, "You can trust me Tomas, I'm on your side, tell me what terrifies the villagers."

A priest in the confessional couldn't be more persuasive.

A reluctant storyteller, Tomas started hesitantly, but remembering what he had witnessed in the last 10-days gave him courage and he opened up,

"I do trust you Lexi, and Carl too, you risked your lives for one of our children, I guess we owe you a true accounting. The cavern existed before the village did, we have always known about it, a mysterious place, religious men visited, and went away in rapture. Many considered it a holy place. Our ancestors told these tales over and over for each new generation."

"The tales darkened when Vlad came here with what was left of his army. He occupied the cavern while his men and the villagers were forced to build his castle; it took years of servitude of the peasant people to finish that evil place."

"During the construction of the castle the villagers learned who he was, his own men were in mortal fear of him, his cruelty had no limits. Little bits at a time, his men let slip what he was running from."

"The Turkish army was going to attack him for his foray into their territory, killing hundreds of innocent villagers as he spread fear and destruction across the land he hoped to annex to his kingdom."

"His terror tactics didn't succeed, and the Turks drove him back to Romania. Through an informer he learned the Turks were gathering a vast army to attack and dethrone him. His castle in Romania was surrounded by woods; he had his army cut down the trees on the outer ring of woods, and sharpened the short stakes left sticking up."

"When the Turkish army came up to his castle, they found more than ten-thousand bodies impaled on the stakes, blocking all approaches. The horses and the men wouldn't go any farther, they retreated, and marched on his brother's castle, his brother didn't put up a fight, he joined the invaders, and fought against Vlad finally usurping his throne. Vlad fled Romania."

"He came here to the Carpathian Mountains, many leagues away from his former kingdom, he was now known as 'Vlad the Impaler'. The castle became a place of debauchery, torture, and sadism."

"People became evermore terrified of it. Then a girl who managed to escape, reported that men in the castle were drinking blood from the necks of unsuspecting travelers, and the legend of Count Dracula was born."

"He surrounded himself with people the same as him. Legend has it that he was a vampire and he turned the others. Before long the countryside was terrorized by more and more vampires, villagers were on guard constantly to protect their families and from a vampire attack."

"The atrocities at the castle degenerated into orgies; using boys from neighboring villages, where unspeakable crimes against nature were committed on them. Rumors circulated that after the most heinous acts were perpetrated on the boys, and blood drained from their necks, their flesh was eaten."

"Help arrived a generation later with a group dedicated to the eradication of all vampires. Every vampire hunter had lost a loved one to a vampire; some even had to destroy the loved one after they had become a vampire."

"Word had reached Sofia, Bulgaria, and Bucharest, Romania of what was going on here. It seems this evil place was spawning vampires to spread their dread disease all over Europe. With Dracula, now well beyond one-hundred, as their leader and would be king over all humanity."

"While groups like the Hunters who came to us were destroying vampires all over Europe, the Doctor who led our Hunters decided it was necessary to cut the head off the monster to stop the spawning of new vampires, and they found their way here. Vlad knew they were here, and why. He carried on a vicious campaign in retaliation for their work killing vampires in Bucharest.

"Over the months of searching for their daytime hiding places, dozens of vampires were staked through the heart, dragged out into the sunlight, or doused with kerosene and set alight. Silver was a valuable tool to use against a vampire, contact with the metal rendered them helpless and burned them as long as the metal was in contact with their skin. Traps were set using silver snares with a person as bait."

"Their numbers were rapidly declining, they never found Vlad however, he hadn't been seen anywhere day or night. The villagers from several villages marched on his castle, what wouldn't burn they tore down and scattered over a wide area. It stayed that way until the government cleaned it up for tourist dollars 35-years ago."

"The local people were freed from the vampire threat, but still nervous because Vlad had never been found. Several decades later strange things began happening in the mountain villages, sheep disemboweled, pets mutilated, visitors waited for never showing up, every week it was a new issue."

"Rumor had it that Vlad didn't leave the area at all; he was in the cavern, hidden in a lower-level crypt where he had been since his castle was torn down. This has been the continuing belief of every villager. Over the years there have been men from the village like the constable, the five goons, as you call them, and the man murdered by his wife. They were enslaved by whatever kind of demon Vlad had transformed into."

"I believe its Vlad and a legion of demons from hell as his handmaidens. They're there; they've been seen, mostly only fleeting glimpses or grotesque shadows, but too many over the years to say its superstition or folktales. We know what the outside world thinks of us, ignorant, superstitious peasants living in the fourteenth century."

Lexis eyes widened in surprise, "Tomas I won't lie to you that is exactly what people think, I did too before I came here, and met you and the others. We know you are no less intelligent than anyone who lives in my neighborhood, Carl and I felt the friendliness from all the first night you asked us to join you in your May Day celebrations. We've been hooked ever since. We're like the Doctor's vampire hunters, we're here to help."

Tomas had tears in his eyes, from frustration or from what Lexi had told him, we weren't sure until he spoke again,

"You two have renewed our faith in the basic goodness of people; I feel that you are going to help us solve this problem."

With Lexi, timing is everything, and he delivered his coup de grace, "Tomas you may have a lot more help very soon, we notified the TV news in Olomouc of the arrests, to get some government action up here, if there's a nest of some ungodly creatures, we're going to need all the help we can get."

At once Tomas relaxed and looked like the jovial inn keeper we first met, "We are going to be in your debt forever," he smiled, "For many years we have tried to get the authorities to help us, they never answered us, and help never arrived. The mountain people have been on their own since the Hunters left, more than 300-years ago."

Tomas fed us and we got ready for the trip back to Brno, I reminded Lexi he had to ask Tomas about Katrina.

"Was the little girl Carl saved a normal child?"

"She was a sweet little thing, considering her father's abuse and her mother's craziness, you'd think she would be messed up in some way, but she was nice girl."

"Does that sound familiar Carl? I'll bet we have another member of the family. I'm going to call Mom."

Mom had been in a state of frenzy waiting for Lexi to call, "It's been hours since you called, I've been frantic with worry, are you and Carl all right? What happened up there, we just heard a report on the TV about some arrests by the Federal Police? Are you involved in that?"

"Mom calm down we're all right, the chief called the TV station in Olomouc to get us some publicity, we're on our way home now, we'll explain everything when we get there. Oh, Tomas told us that Katrina was a very nice, normal little girl. Bye."

We loaded our gear, and the security guards in the van, and headed back to Brno, feeling like we had accomplished the goals we set for today even if we had more questions that needed answers. Once on the road Lexi began discussing what Tomas had told us of the history pertaining to the cavern and the village.

The chief gave us his take on the story, "I'm not one to see spooks around every corner and vampires don't exist, but something is terrorizing these people, and it has something to do with that cavern."

"I agree Chief," Lexi came back, "The villagers have witnessed the carnage, and suffered from the loss of loved ones, mutilated animals, and pets slaughtered, one on the hood of our car. That's enough to get my blood boiling, do you want to come back next week?"

"I sure do," he replied, "If you need my men they're available too, we can adjust schedules and give the rest of the security guards some overtime. The men here are as outraged by the constable and his goons as I was, almost all are former police or military, so we know how to handle ourselves in tight situations."

"You're part of our investigation then chief; we'll discuss all plans with you for your perspective and recommendations. This was scheduled as a 2-day operation, we want to pay you and the men for the 2-days, after what we went through, you deserve hazard pay, we should talk about that, think it over and get back to me."

We parted at Mom and Dad's house with assurances of communications between us soon. Mom was out the door before we had a chance to knock, hugging us both at the same time, relief written all over her face.

"Thank God you're all right, I was worried sick. Come in and tell us all about it," she demanded as she pushed us into the entry hall where Dad appeared on his way from the library.

"I was on the phone with a psychiatrist on the Medical Board, he's the lead doctor in the review of Katrina's case," he could barely contain his excitement, "I told him what you related to your mother, Its almost a sure thing now that we'll get the visa."

Good news all over, I was elated, we could do something for this mistreated child; maybe she'll have a chance for a normal life.

Sitting at the kitchen table for 2-hours we retold the story in every detail, and answered a hundred questions, they thought we were too hasty informing the press of the arrests, there would be consequences they opined.

"That's what we want," Lexi exclaimed, "We felt if they hid this incident like the first one, we would spin our wheels for months."

"I've been working on a story for my publishers, and I've come up with a zinger of an idea." I said, instant attention followed, as I laid out my plan,

"Tomas is not an ignorant peasant, I find him well informed, and articulate, he's an autodidactic if ever there was one. I want him to explain the happenings in the village, and his reaction to the lack of assistance from the authorities. How they view the outside world, and what they think of our opinion of them, just to mention a few subjects."

"I think we should do it as an interview, Lexi will ask him questions, leading questions, of course, and let him vent his spleen. We'll video it and I'll write up the interview in English, strictly using his own words."

"If it carries any punch we can have Lexi translate it into Czech, and send it to the editorial director of every newspaper, TV, and radio station, in the Czech Republic. The news release of the arrest will be the precursor of the story."

The kitchen was silent for a second or two, then all three started speaking at once, Lexi being the loudest, was the one I heard,

"That is the best idea I've heard all week. If we get the story out for everybody to see, the government can't cover it up, they'll be forced to take some action."

Mom and Dad didn't think it would work, "Most people couldn't care less, if there's no public outcry where will you be?"

"We'll just have to make it extra special heartrending, show pictures of the cavern with the altar and the iron rings set into the wall; no one is going to mistake that for anything but what it is. If that doesn't work, then at least we tried, we can't just sit around and do nothing."

I hoped to convince them; four heads together can devise some brilliant ideas.

Mom was the first to give in, she sighed, "Those poor people. You and Lexi can help? How can two of you take on a force that they couldn't destroy for 3-centuries?"

Dad didn't like the implication that Mom believed the vampire nonsense, "Barbara you're not falling for that superstitious hogwash are you?"

Mom returned just as pointed as he had been, "There's something there that's deeply disturbing for those people, and you don't know any more than I do, so don't call me superstitious."

"Dad, she's got a point, until we know what it is that's causing the mayhem, we're all in the dark, that's why the idea Carl has is so good, it'll force the issue into the spotlight and maybe we can get a look at 'it', whatever 'it' is. Can we keep an open mind, and brainstorm a strategy to illuminate the dark corners?"

Lexi can charm his parents as he charms everyone; I guess no one is immune.

Mom complained that dinner was going to be a disaster because she was so distraught while preparing it. She couldn't remember if she put in all the ingredients the recipe called for. She must have been on autopilot; the chicken cacciatore with fettuccini was up to her impeccable standards.

After dinner we discussed the future, Katrina, and other noncontroversial subjects, until Mom declared the day had been so stressful that she was exhausted. We decided to retire, but before we stood, Lexi squeezed my hand, and I immediately got hard, he was signaling what was coming next.

We entered the bedroom; Lexi put his arms around me and kissed me with his usual passion,

"I love you Carl," he whispered in my ear.

I was a goner. He could have asked me to forfeit my life for him, and I would have. He's everything I dreamed of, and everything I wanted, there would never be anyone who could replace this paragon of beauty and virtue.

"I love you too, Lexi." I managed to get out, emotion choking me up.

We caressed each other standing by the bed, and slowly, while kissing, unbuttoned each other's shirt, and pants, stripping us naked. In each other's arms we fell to the bed, Lexis passion seemed more demanding than it had ever been.

I put his cock in the crack of my ass, and we slid his cock on my ass and my cock on his belly until it became unbearable, and we had to go to the next level. I asked if he wanted to fuck me, and he made a garbled response that I took for a yes. I turned to him, and put his cock on my sphincter, I wanted to pleasure my lover. We used no lubricant but the precum leaking from the slit in his cock, he entered me as I had entered him, and we were one.

I had never craved anal sex, being the bottom anyway, but my lover seemed to know what to do, I wanted his beautiful cock to stay in my ass forever. We had passionate sex two more times that night. After each climax I wondered how I could live without this, he controlled my present and my future.

CHAPTER 12

TO KILL A VAMPIRE

Indeed, there were consequences. We learned during brunch on Sunday morning; the Federal Justice Ministry in a live interview, issued a statement that reported the arrest of five local mountain men charged with inciting an insurrection against a legally sanctioned study group.

The report insinuated the five men were only against the hydroelectric plant planned for the river's waterfall, and attempted to impede the group's work. The village constable was also arrested and charged with dereliction of duty by the local Moravian District Authority.

Lexi was furious, "They're doing it again, and it'll be stuffed in a 'confidential' file and never seen again. We gave the police statements that we would have been assassinated if we hadn't been advised to watch for just what happened. Yet there are no charges of attempted murder, conspiracy to commit murder, or possession of firearms by unlicensed individuals."

"They are going to play this as a political protest," Dad announced, "It's of no benefit to the government to start an investigation of monsters that the people don't believe exist. I'm not so sure they won't hold these criminals while they try to find out what their goals are, they know it's not just a political protest, there was no fanfare about the study, or public notices of intention to build a hydroelectric plant."

"Anybody going into this mess without an open mind will come up with just more questions, as we did before we ever set foot in the

Carpathians," I said, trying to make it sound logical, "There are more things in heaven and earth, Horatio than are dreamt of in your philosophy." I quoted, "Shakespeare was speaking of ghosts, it's impossible to prove they don't exist, like the villager's monster, you can't prove a negative."

"Do you believe in vampires Carl?" Mom asked, "Do we arm you two with wooden stakes, holy water, crucifixes, and a necklace of garlic bulbs?"

"Sarcasm isn't going to work either Mom, Carl is not willing to rule anything out before we have a clue to what it might be. The point is," Lexi emphasized, "something is there, we have to discover what."

"I'm sorry Carl, if that sounded sarcastic," Mom said contritely, "I was trying to show how ill equipped you are for fighting shadows."

"No apology necessary Mom, we're not well equipped, but we're going to be by the time we go back."

"What do you know of vampire strengths and weaknesses?" Dad suddenly asked, "From legend I mean, and fictional accounts."

"Just what I've read, for a while as a teenager I was obsessed with the romantic notion of vampires' immortality, rather benign beings, except when forced to feed. I read all the books by Ann Rice, and many others."

"The standard weaknesses are; the sun, vulnerability during the day while sleeping, Moms remedies, garlic, holy water, crucifixes and wooden stakes. Their strengths; immortality, superhuman strength, speed, mind control, sensory perception, and cunning."

"Tomas told us yesterday that silver was a major weapon used against them. Otherwise, we stand in ignorance." I finished, feeling a little foolish, like a teenager again.

"That's where we start then; you know all the traditional vulnerabilities, plan to utilize them, research nontraditional methods to destroy them, like silver. What does silver do to a vampire?" Dad asked.

"It renders them helpless, and burns them constantly while their skin is in contact with it, according to legend. Tomas told us, it was used to rid the area of all the monsters except Vlad, who disappeared. I'll ask him how they utilized it, probably chains made of silver," Lexi responded, "He said they used traps with human bait, we'll have him elaborate on that too."

Mom was a little skeptical, "This is a strange conversation, everything you have suggested sounds like in-close fighting, why can't we use silver bullets, or fragmenting hand-grenades filled with silver pellets?"

"How about a canister of silver oxide mixed with a liquid that's insoluble to the oxide and a high-pressure spray device? There's also silver fulminate, it's highly explosive but can be handled effectively in small amounts. You can't try get close to anything so repulsive."

"That is exactly what I meant; everything Mom has suggested is definitely nontraditional, and probably effective for not getting too close." Dad admiringly commented, "Barbara, what the hell is silver fulminate?"

"A very unstable, highly explosive compound, the smallest pressure, even a leaf falling on a small amount, causes a very large explosion; it's used in tiny concentrations in children's noise makers." Mom explained,

"I learned about it in basic chemistry, and thought that even though it's difficult to work with, small amounts a little larger than the amount in a noise maker could be strategically placed to explode when someone stepped on it. Lay down on it, as in a coffin, and the silver particles penetrating their skin would be deadly, the explosion wouldn't be lethal to people,

"You're really getting into this aren't you?" Lexi asked Mom, "I think you believe this a bit."

"I read vampire stories too Lexi, they seemed real, once it's in your head it stays there. I'm continuing the stories with my plot and solutions. Isn't that what we agreed to do, keep an open mind, think outside the box, and come up with nontraditional ideas?"

"I'm teasing Mom," Lexi laughed, "Your ideas are great, I'm not too keen on getting close to a monster." Prophetic words to be sure.

"We have to find a chemist for the gas seepage; he may be able to elaborate on Mom's ideas." I said, "I like the idea of putting a silver bomb in the coffin, it would be a trip to watch it, but the silver oxide idea is better. Acting as a pepper spray, we wouldn't have to get too close, and if there's more than one of them it'll be a lot easier than stakes."

Mom jumped up from the table, "Enough of this subject for today, there's a band concert in Brno at Linkin Park at 3:00 p.m., and we're going, move it."

We took the Audi so Lexi could show Mom and Dad what a great vehicle it was, they were duly impressed. The band concert was impressive also, the change of pace gave us a chance to take a break from the gruesome business of inventing ways to kill vampires.

Linkin Park is every bit as pretty as Central Park in New York, magical fountains, beautiful statuary, tall graceful trees and immaculate walkways. We strolled around the park after the concert enjoying the advent of spring, blossoming flowers, and leaves coming back on the trees, it was a warm, May Sunday afternoon, lulling us, while evil was running amok in our valley.

Dinner at an outdoor café bordering the park fulfilled the promise of a family after 25-years, overriding the anguish, and trepidation of the past week. Mom and Dad tried and succeeded in making me feel one of the family, for the first time in my life I saw what true parenting was; unconditional love, and acceptance, utterly foreign to me.

Lexi sensed my confusion, and on the way home held my hand, gently squeezing it, telling me he understood. We made love that night, slow, and sweet, this boy could read a person's mood without trying, it was a natural gift, I thanked the universal powers for bringing us together.

Monday morning dawned bright and cloudless, a good omen one might say, but a call to the cell phone we gave to Tomas proved that assumption false. Reprisals had gone to lengths that even the government couldn't cover with sugar, an orgy of killing of farm animals and pets, and barns burned. In an urban setting such violence on a comparative basis would be justification for martial law.

However, as usual, the government was silent. Mom and Dad finally saw the situation as the authorities only covering their asses. They enthusiastically joined our mission to rid the River Town of the inherent evil pervading the everyday life of these good people. Dad gave in first, only because Mom was still too stunned to respond,

"I can't understand why there's not a massive infusion of federal troops to quell what appears to be an assault on civil authority. What justification can they possibly use to absolve themselves of responsibility?"

Lexi, my diplomat, spoke up at once, "They are the final word, for us to complain will be futile. Do you see the wisdom of having Tomas make a statement on video now? It may change or at least influence the prevailing attitudes at the Ministry of Justice, and hopefully the public."

"We must have done something to upset it," I thought aloud, "The goons must have been the eyes and ears for him, or it, in the village, we cut off its information, and it's pissed. Is there a way we can use this to our advantage?"

"Look at it from a work perspective," Dad said, "When you lose all your workers, you shut down, as in a strike or a natural disaster. That's what happened here, now he has to recruit new workers to stay on top of events and plans in the village, especially with outside interference from us."

"The important question is how it chooses its daytime protectors, if that's what they are. From the limited knowledge we have, it seems that all five of the goons were arrogant, had a bullying nature, were troublemakers, and drank too much. They believed they could take liberties, as the one who sexually abused his 4-year-old daughter. It's not much to go on, but it's all we have."

"Assuming mind control is the way he bends these men to do his will, I think it only follows that a logical pattern of superiority is planted in their minds, probably by hypnosis, all five were alike in that regard, and the constable. To replace his drones he will have to recruit from the men of the villages."

"Tomas can be very helpful by watching for signs of change; I presume it will be a one at a time selection. The first one Tomas suspects to be in its power, we feed him false information, it would be a huge advantage."

Lexi's professor called with better news, he had spoken with a high-ranking official at the Ministry of Justice. Dad was right, they were investigating, and the five goons would stay in custody until a decision was made on what to charge them with.

They requested we finish our preliminary study as quickly as possible to forestall any further civil disobedience. The Professor informed them of the caverns below being a possible weakness for the floor of the main cavern chamber.

The number of smaller chambers down there, the possibility of illegal activity in the cavern, and more assassins waiting in ambush were also discussed. The official made a couple of calls and arranged for an armed swat team of 20-men to clear the caverns so we could do our study.

An appointment was set up with a geologist and a sonic technician who did microgravity surveys, Karst related, which is sound waves used to discover hidden tunnels, caves, mines, and underground water filled cavities leading to sink holes.

The geologist would map the entire cave system and video all the chambers, he also worked on underground gas seepage usually radon, but his instruments would show if there were gases of any nature in the cavern, and in what concentrations.

Wednesday was set for the swat team and geology team. A small sample of gas discovered would suffice for a chemist and a toxicologist to make a finding, no need to have them onsite.

"The speed of this operation is definitely increasing," Lexi observed, "Now we have to keep the pressure on whatever entity is in the cavern, and with a little luck, force it into the open. One way to keep the government involved is for you," he said looking at me, "To write the article that's going to give the village some much needed publicity."

"When Tomas was telling us the trouble the village has experienced, did he say the crimes were reported and to whom?" I asked, "I have an idea for the video interview. We have to research any reported crimes or mutilations, missing persons, and any other reported incident, would the reports be in Olomouc?"

"He said the constable made all such reports, Olomouc is the seat of the district, so any reports would be there, if the constable even made the reports. What's your idea Carl, spill it?"

"I thought that we could have a list of reported crimes and dates running as a banner under the video of Tomas as proof that his claims had been vetted. The crimes were reported, but not followed up by anyone in authority."

"That would work if reports actually reached Olomouc," He reasoned, "I'm afraid we may be disappointed by that line of inquiry. The constable was one of the goons; I doubt he was conscientiously doing his job."

"When you call the chief ask him to check it out, he knows people in the Olomouc police community perhaps he can find something," Mom said, "It may work, it would be a powerful tool if there's any record."

Lexi called the chief, and set up a meeting for later in the afternoon, we met in the security office at the hospital. We related all the plans we had for taking out any creatures, vampires, or otherwise, the video we planned to make, and involve Tomas in playing detective.

"I agree with almost everything, I can't get into the vampire thing, it's bizarre." Loic said.

Lexi, did his open mind speech again, "Chief, we're not saying there is or isn't such creatures, we have agreed between ourselves to keep an open mind in order to solve what **is** up there, you admit yourself that it's scary the way someone knows our every move."

"If you had seen the room under the main cavern with the blood soaked altar and the iron rings set into the walls, you wouldn't be as skeptical." I said, "More rooms are down there, but we didn't think it would be a smart move to search them with only four of us, and no means to defend ourselves."

"Would it hurt to prepare for it being real? If it's not, there's no harm done, we just feel foolish, if there's an element of truth in it, we're prepared to protect ourselves."

"Could you supply us with some of the ammunition you use in your handguns so we can have them coated with silver? It's the same whether they're coated or not. Your weapon is a 9-millimeter Luger isn't it?" The chief nodded in the affirmative, "Are all you weapons Lugers?" he nodded again, "Then we will have some clips made up for your 9-millimeter's, silver coated, you don't even have to tell your men if you don't want to, just a precaution."

"Did you go to school to be a con man or something?" the chief asked, "You could sell refrigerators to the Eskimos. Okay, I'm on board as long as you don't insist I believe this crap."

"What can you do on the reports thing? Mom said you knew People in Olomouc, can you make a call to see if the constable filed reports?"

"I'll do better than that I'll go up to Olomouc tomorrow, and have lunch with my police academy buddy who happens to be the chief of police. He'll open any doors I need opened."

Tuesday was a very busy day; we purchased 40-clips of 9-millimeter ammunition, talked a jeweler into silver coating them, and paid an outrageous price because we wouldn't tell him what they were for.

Six battery operated video spy cams were bought for the cavern, all programmed to the same receiver, with motion sensor operation.

Purchasing silver oxide was a little more difficult, so we enlisted Mom with a medical professional's credentials to grease the way. Then explained to a chemist, who incidentally thought we were crazy, to make us a solution that would be insoluble for the silver oxide, and found a pressurized canister as a way of disbursing it. A productive day indeed, we felt somewhat more secure than yesterday.

Tuesday evening the chief called with the best news we could have expected. The constable had filed dozens of reports in the 7-years he was the village constable, all were available.

Loic went the extra mile and paid a worker in the district office to separate the River Town reports from other mountain villages, put them in chronological order, and send them to him at the hospital, 20-year's worth of reports.

Our spirits were high as we ate dinner and created a scenario for the video recording. Dubbing voices versus subtitles, and how many different languages to translate the initial video into, the original would be in Czech.

We wanted it to go viral throughout the European Union, which meant Italian, Czech, Spanish, English, and French. Although there's more languages in the EU, the five mentioned covered most of the people in Europe. First I had to write an article, actually a full-length feature story covering my original mission. If I didn't give my publishers the scoop, I'd be blackballed from writing for years.

Dad speculated on the news from the chief, "As I mentioned before, those goons were arrogant, probably under posthypnotic suggestion; anything they did was, in their mind unassailable by anyone."

"The constable felt he could do his job, and report all incidents with impunity. It worked, there never was an investigation, his master was never threatened, our gain and his master's downfall."

We pored over the police reports.

CHAPTER 13

DEMONS FROM HELL

Chief rented the same 8-passenger van as before, and came to get us. We headed to the cavern, determined to learn the truth of what existed in the labyrinth beneath the river.

No one was in sight at the rear entrance to the cavern, so we waited for the others to arrive. The Professor showed up with his crew 10-minutes later, followed shortly by the geological team that stopped on the other side of the bridge, and exited the vehicle.

Curiosity spurred us toward the bridge where the head of the team was pointing out to his men the geological features of the area under and around the bridge. The outcropping, he explained, at a time millions of years ago, extended across the river where the bridge presently stands.

A mammoth lake was behind the outcropping, which effectively blocked the ravine. He pointed to the erosion marks high on the ravine walls; this was a cataract as big as the one below it now. He opined that an underground conduit beneath the lake created the caverns behind the falls, carving its way through the rock over millennia.

He said a fault ran the length of the Western range of the Carpathian Mountains. Many eons ago an earthquake caused the outcropping to collapse into the underground passages. Billions of gallons of water stored behind it, and up the ravine were released. The present waterfall was created, and the cavern sealed from the river's underground path.

The lesson in geology was interesting, but it brought up a question, which had to be answered if a hydroelectric station was to be built on this river. How much erosion did the underground river cause, was the rock under the second-sub-level riddled with more caverns?

The answer was waiting for us in the cavern. The arrival of the Federal swat team, as all government agencies that work by their own clock, showed up an hour late, just as we were preparing to go in alone with only our guards. With no explanation or apology, just a 'let's get this done', we headed through the laurel thicket, and into the cavern.

As the geological team set up their lights and equipment, the police searched every corner of the main level, they found nothing. With lights illuminating the stairway down to the lower-level, they went single file crouched in fighting stance with weapons in kill mode.

In the chamber with the altar, which the other chambers opened from, they regrouped, and like a drill team split into five groups. One group for each passageway they proceeded into the tunnels with lights on their weapons and helmets illuminating the way.

When they left the room we realized the altar was no longer there, and no sign of it ever being there. The altar was solid rock, one piece that large would weigh tons, the dried blood may have disguised the fact of individual blocks but improbable.

While the sonic technicians ran their microgravity survey, the guards stood at the entrance to each tunnel with their weapons drawn, but not aiming down the tunnels. Ten-minutes had passed when we heard a gunshot in the tunnels, seconds ticked by and we heard two more shots.

The chief was clearly concerned, and wanted to go into the tunnel system. Discretion held sway, and he stayed alert and ready for anything that might come out, but declined to go in. The squad began to exit the tunnels, all accounted for, Sergeant Dvorak, head of the squad, questioned the reason for the shooting.

Four officers who had gone down the furthest tunnel from the stairs answered; they had seen movement in one of the chambers, a warning shot was fired, an animal of some strange species ran from the chamber.

Two of the men shot it, and it continued around a turn, when they got to the turn it was nowhere in sight. Searching the other chambers past the turn, they found nothing, just chambers full of bones. Another of the four-man teams had found a partially decomposed body of an adult male.

Their own medical examiners would check those remains and the bones found in almost all the chambers. The stench in these chambers was the overpowering smell of death; however, in one slightly larger chamber the stench was animal, straw bedding on the floor indicated more than one animal in residence. The connecting tunnels were searched, and no animals found.

When they joined the groups from the other 4-entrances, no other animal sightings were reported, just the one, and all four officers swore it had been hit twice; it had jerked forward on both shots, and should be dead.

As the police gave the chief their report, it made me wonder whether there could be a hidden exit from these tunnels. More lighting was needed, air pumped in to push the stench out, decomposing bodies removed, and the piles of bones examined to determined whether they were animal or human, then we could look for another exit.

A cleanup would occur at some point, and clear up any vanishing animal mystery, the sooner the better. Lexi, the chief, and I, went over the police report, the chief was having some doubts about the validity of his convictions.

"What kind of animal runs on two legs except a primate? They swore it was not an ape, it looked to some degree human."

"Another mystery is where did it disappear to?" I said, "There has to be another exit or a hidden chamber, I want this place sanitized and electric lighting installed to see exactly what is here."

Lexi found a quick solution, "I'll call Dad, and have him arrange for a cleanup company to bring the electrical equipment and the pumps to at least make the air breathable. Even while the coroner is here they can be installing lights in the tunnels."

"The coroner might show this afternoon," the chief replied, "The police squad is staying on to investigate exactly what criminal enterprise was conducted here. They'll be here for a few days."

Meanwhile, the geology team continued mapping the tunnels, videotaping every opening, twist, and turn, taking sonic soundings every few feet. They found no cavities below the tunnels.

The area completed first was the upper chamber, the sounding of the floor found it had an average of 12-feet of solid granite, one major roadblock avoided. The Professor pronounced shortly after 12-noon that the cavern was safe to install machinery.

We stopped for lunch, brought in by the police, compliments of the Ministry of Justice.

"I spoke with Dad; he's going to arrange a cleanup for tomorrow morning, he's coming with them." Lexi reported, "Do you think we should discourage him from coming, it could become a dangerous place to be, and he's not exactly a spring chicken?"

"He's old enough to make his own decisions Lexi, we'll keep him close, and make sure he's safe, don't fret about it, I'm going to help, remember? Did he say why he wanted to come up here?"

"He thinks it'll help for him to analyze the stories of Tomas and others, to make sure the video will be as credible as it will need to be." Lexi replied, "It's not a bad idea I just don't want him getting hurt."

"I bet he feels the same way about you, maybe he wanted to be here to protect you, in case you fall off the teeter-totter." I joked, "He'll be bringing Band-Aids too, in case you skin your knees."

"You're going to pay for that crack Carl, we'll have payback tonight." Lexi retorted, "But now I have some news from the Professor, he agrees with you about a hidden room or a secret exit. So he directed the sonic technicians to sound the outer walls of the lower caverns. We should know something by tomorrow morning."

"How is the gas seepage problem?" I asked.

"They haven't started on it yet. The physical stability of the floor was their primary concern, then the fear of honeycombing under the lower level and now the outer walls. They intend to do that tomorrow I guess, because the Professor said they would be finished by tomorrow."

"The chief's men are installing the motion sensing cameras now in 6-locations where any traffic has to pass in order to get in or out. Whether we are here or nearby we can view it in real time, otherwise, whatever the hell that thing is, will be recorded."

"The police don't know we're putting them in there, if they know, and there's anything on the tape, they will seize it as evidence. Then bury it so they don't have to explain what kind of creature it is, and how it came to be here in the mountains."

Lexi was excited at the prospect of a positive outcome; we might overcome decades of what bedeviled the villagers. Good times were right around the corner. The corner, alas, was nowhere in sight.

Places to stay were not plentiful in the small mountain villages; the police had brought two large mobile home type trailers. They were bunked in very cramped circumstances, competing for sleeping space with their gear, communication equipment, and weapons, still better than sleeping in the cavern.

Tomas had rooms for the guard, Lexi, and me; the Professor, his crew, and the geology team were relegated to nearby villages. No one had to drive through the mountains at night.

Tomas served us dinner whipped up at the last minute; the man's a true hotelier as worthy of that title as any 5-star hotel in Prague. Chicken stew with dumplings may not rank at the top of a gourmet menu at the

Majestic Hotel, but according to 14-hungry men it was hot, filling, and delicious, he received no complaints.

The Professor and his men left for the inn in the adjacent village, the geology team had left before dinner for a town a few miles away. A card game began, the men in good spirits considering the events of the day.

The chief sat with Lexi and me at a table away from the game so we could talk without being overheard. The chief began,

"These SWAT teams are all handpicked veteran police officers, sharpshooting is mandatory in their line of work it means the life of a hostage or a fellow officer. So when they say the animal was hit twice, I don't question that for one minute. How would it continue running with two bullets in it? I know what comes next, you are going to tell me, the next encounter with whatever it was, we will use the silver bullets, is that a correct assumption?"

"You're getting there chief, what do we have to lose?" Lexi grinned, "I'm more worried about our cameras and lights being destroyed, if it activates a camera, the security light comes on, don't you think the creature would try to get rid of the light if not the camera?"

"It's a hazard we have to live with; a camera without lights is useless, unless it's a night vision camera and those are pretty much obvious to anyone. If the light is destroyed we will still have the animal videoed, we can always change a light, and it's the cameras that have to be unnoticed."

I thought the chief must have been a spy in a previous life, he's thorough and sharp.

"Is there a way we could send tear gas or something through the tunnels," Lexi inquired, "Or is there a knockout gas? That sounds illegal, doesn't it? But we have to clear the tunnels and chambers for the place to be sealed if there is gas seepage."

"The police and the army are the only ones authorized to use tear gas, and that's for riot control, I'll ask Dvorak if it's possible, don't get your hopes up. As for knockout gas, you're on the mark, it is illegal."

We went over our plans for the next day, then watched the game for a while and when I had trouble keeping my eyes open, Lexi suggested we call it a night. The chief left with us, admonishing his men not to be playing cards all night, we said goodnight at his door, which was next to our room.

"So much for sex tonight," I commented ruefully, "These walls are paper thin, I can hear him moving around like he's in this room."

"Don't fret, as you put it, you're not getting any sex tonight anyway," Lexi gleefully remarked, "Pay back's a bitch, I warned you."

I grabbed him before he could gloat some more and kissed him with a force he didn't expect, "Then I'll be the caveman, and not bother to ask" I said kissing him again. We laughed, and for the first time since the river dunking, we slept in separate beds, neither of us with enough self-control to keep our hands off each other.

Tuesday morning was gray and wet; last night's high spirits had vanished. After a short conference with Dvorak, he gave us the same answer as the chief had,

"If we locate someone, or something that we can't flush out by regular methods then we'll use tear gas. I like the plan to circulate clean air into the tunnels it'll make our work easier too, I'm sure the coroner will thank you, they have the worst smelling job there is."

We waited for the coroner and his forensic team before starting any work in the tunnels, but we checked the videotapes when the police had gone to the lower level to make a sweep before anyone was allowed in.

"There it is," Lexi yelled, "It worked, what the hell is that thing?" he stopped short, we couldn't believe what we were seeing, for a few seconds we had a picture of a creature straight out of hell, the thing ripped the light off the wall, and the video went black.

"Go back, go back," Lexi was excitedly shouting, we replayed the short segment over and over, but got no closer to identifying the abomination. I tried to describe what we were seeing; it had the general

153

shape of a human, head, two legs, two arms, and a torso, all similarities ended there.

Its skin looked like slimy, wet leather stretched tight; the eyes were protruding at least one inch from the sockets and had only large black pupils. It had no nose, just a hole above a larger hole that one filled with small pointed teeth like a shark. No ears, no hair, no neck, the head was a continuation of the torso, sloped shoulders that had two appendages hanging apelike to the floor.

The whole body twisted grotesquely, Lexi compared it to a pretzel. I will never again eat a pretzel; it will only conjure up the nightmare we were seeing on the screen.

A monstrous phallus hung between its legs, too large for the body it was on, bigger than the arm, and it too almost dragging on the floor. Revolting is a word that comes to mind to describe the twisted body and phallus. The hand that reached up to tear the light off the wall was easily the most human feature on the body. It had long slim fingers and thumb, slightly gnarled but identifiable as human, but this was no primate.

Chief was speechless, "I can't believe something like that could exist, it took two bullets and didn't drop, is it real? My god, having that thing touch you would drive a person insane."

"I just remembered something Tomas told you," I said, "Didn't he say the demons from hell were glimpsed briefly over the centuries? It meets all the requirements of a demon from hell, and I'm not sure it isn't. No wonder the people are terrified, I am, and if you two are honest you'll admit you are too." The chief and Lexi just nodded their heads.

With the horror of the video still at the front of our minds, we went to see how other matters were progressing. The sonic technicians were waiting for the police to complete their sweep of the tunnels before moving the sound generators and monitors to the lower level.

The geologists were making the most of the wait by doing a preliminary check for gas. Their instruments were showing gas in small amounts, but in different areas of the main cavern, the geologist speculated that there were vents coming from some lower chambers, the real test would be down there.

Video recordings made the day before were poorly lit, and details weren't clearly defined, but it gave us an idea how extensive this labyrinth was, and what a huge job it promised to be clearing it out.

Midmorning, Dad and two huge trucks arrived loaded with exhaust fans, suction fans, 12-inch diameter flex ducts, temporary lighting, as used when a new Egyptian tomb is discovered, scaffolding, generators, and garbage cans. They unloaded the trucks, and started stretching out the flex duct, we decided to bring fresh air in from the water curtain side, it was closest.

Ducted air would blow up to the gallery where there were openings to the outside, saving ducting and work to carry the exhaust all the way to the laurel grove. The company Dad hired was a disaster cleanup outfit, and they knew their business.

Minutes after unloading we heard the generators start, and shortly after, the powerful fins of the suction fan from the rear entrance side of the cavern howled with fetid air being sucking into the ducts. Exhaust fans were bringing fresh air in from the water curtain side. The police in the tunnels were shouting their thanks, fresh air, such a simple concept appreciated way out of proportion to its monetary value.

No incidents in the tunnels or lower chambers today, the police finished their sweep, and gave the okay for our workers to enter, except for the chamber with the corpse of the adult male.

The sonic crew was first in the central lower chamber, the plan was to work their away around the tunnel system sending sound waves into the outer walls of the caverns.

They started at the first entrance to the right of the staircase, in the first chamber tested; they had readouts that indicated a void behind the supposed outer wall. Pandemonium ensued, guards geologists, police,

I guess everybody, crowded into the chamber, well lit by this time, and breathable.

The chamber was 20-feet from the entrance to the opposite wall, and about 40-feet wide. The wall was on an odd angle in relation to the outer chamber and the tunnel, as if a wall had been erected to block one corner of the room.

No evidence of a false wall was found though, it was solid rock. Disappointed we went back to our individual endeavors, wondering what was behind the rock, and whether it was accessible.

The coroner was an officious little man, barely 5-foot tall, but with an ego about 6-foot-6. Aggravated beyond reason that we were in the tunnels, he expounded on the inefficiency of the police, the advisability of our study, and how he was going to rectify our clumsy handling of this investigation. I suggested to Lexi that we show him our video of the creature and watch him shit his little pants.

We held our peace and let him do his job hoping it would be over and done with quickly. His first pronouncement informed us that the murder of the male corpse was not committed here. Duh!

He didn't elaborate on the cause or the condition of the body, but demanded that the bones in the adjoining chambers be packed for transportation to his labs. There, he would determine whether they were human or animal, and whether we had compromised his investigation.

A world-class jerk; he was the object of scorn for all present. Then he left, the place could be cleared out, cleaned up, and deodorized.

Where did the creature that we had on video, disappear to so quickly? Was this demon from hell a supernatural entity that could disappear at will? All these questions had to be answered before this project could move forward.

Chief stated his position, "I think we should show the police the video and maybe they will use tear gas to clear the caverns."

"But chief, the creature is nowhere in the caverns," I said, "what good will tear gas do if there's another exit down here? I don't believe in its supernatural abilities, I think it has survival abilities, which means it has a way to avoid us. We have to be realistic, there are no supernatural vanishing acts, let's be more diligent in finding other means of exiting these caverns."

We revisited the first cavern going over every inch of the outer wall; there were no openings, no evidence of movable walls, nothing.

Chapter 14

Supernatural Disappearing Act

The geologist, who gave us the lesson of how the caverns were created, came down the stairs from the upper chamber with a smug look on his face,

"I've been pondering your dilemma, and I figured it out," he pronounced, "The void behind that wall continues back under the stairs. We can't get a reading from the stairs themselves, they're too thick; the stairs were carved into solid rock."

"I asked our technician to take a reading in the chamber to the right, on the wall under the stairs, not the outer wall; he's on his way back here."

We excitedly hurried to the other chamber, and the technician was just starting his sound probe, 2-minutes later, proved the geologist correct, there was a void under the stairs. We yelled for Dad to get his crew to give us some lights, and soon we were seeing this chamber clearly for the first time. About the same size as its next-door neighbor but without the odd angled wall. It also had recessed niches set into the walls around the chamber; one niche was in the wall under the stairs.

The geologist pointed proudly at the niche and said,

"Gentlemen, the entrance to the void in the rock. I have a theory about this; the tunnels run all the way under the river to the bridge. When the rock outcropping collapsed into the ravine where the bridge is now, it sealed the caverns from any further water penetration. At this spot we are halfway to the bridge, between here and the bridge you might find another exit, and there's likely more than one."

We examined the niche carefully, and there were faint lines around the perimeter of the space, for this to be a door the mason who built it must have been at the top of his trade. First we had to discover whether it was a door; there was no evidence of a hidden catch or lever on or near the niche.

Lexi and the geologist were working methodically inch by inch away from the niche in both directions. Within a few feet from the entrance corner of the chamber, the geologist found a small opening starting at the floor and up the wall.

Reminiscent of a cartoon mouse hole, it was roughly 3-inches-high, and 3-inches-wide. One-inch-deep in the hole something was blocking it, not stone, it looked like metal, he tapped it with the toe of his shoe, and silently the niche swung open.

Revealed was a staircase heading up, at least 6-feet wide, approximately 200-feet farther up the stairs was dim daylight, as if they made a 90-degree turn. We made a mad rush to the opening to find the location of the exit.

Lexi was first, and burst out of the opening 100-feet from the bridge, and 10-feet above the river, a rock ledge ran along the river and under the bridge, but there was no way up the steep rock sides of the riverbank.

Leaving the destination of the ledge for another time, we returned to the latest alternate entrance, it wasn't concealed at all, and it couldn't be seen from the bridge or the road.

I stopped at the niche door to examine how it opened and closed. The mechanism was simplicity personified, the rock door was so perfectly balanced that when the trip bar was pushed, the stop moved enough for the door to swing open. When the door was pushed to close it, the stop popped up and held the door closed. Ingenious, was this the work of Vlad or the mystics who predated him by a few centuries?

The discovery of another exit didn't satisfy me, the geologist's words kept coming back, 'there's likely more exits'. I went to find the technicians. They were more than halfway around the perimeter of the tunnel system and had discovered no more voids, solid rock so far.

I tried to picture the riverbank on the opposite side of the river from where we found the latest opening. My mental picture of it was a low rock wall from the water to the pastures above. It seemed unlikely the farmers who pastured their sheep there would do so with a doorway to hell nearby.

The disaster cleanup company had all the tunnels and chambers lighted, and looking normal. The fetid air was going fast, still far from being fresh air, but it was breathable without worrying whether your breakfast was going to come back up.

The geologist did another round of videotaping the tunnels and chambers, now we could see how this place was configured. The chamber at the foot of the stairs was almost the center of the lower-level; five tunnels ran out from this hub, two from the side with the stairs and three around perimeter on the opposite side.

The tunnel on the right of the stairs ran toward the bridge, up to a solid rock wall, and followed the wall to the other side of the cavern, then turned back toward the falls. This side of the lower-level was wider than the stair side, and had one more tunnel interchanging with the bridge end tunnel, and turned back to join the falls end tunnel.

Six chambers were on the perimeter wall on the stair side, four to the left and two to the right, 7-chambers were on the opposite perimeter side connected with each other and with the tunnels. In the center were

18-chambers, some the size of a large closet, most with two or more openings joining other chambers or a tunnel.

Many rooms had the same iron rings fastened into the rock as the main lower chamber, obviously cells. The geologist had to spray paint numbers on the entrances to the many randomly located chambers; the maze was very confusing.

They discovered a void in the last chamber on the side opposite the stairs; it appeared to be directly under where Lexi and I first entered the cavern. It struck me that the blind wall by the curtain of water could be also a way up to the pasture land.

Armed with lights and slickers Lexi and I investigated both sides of the blind wall. On the cavern side there was nothing but solid rock, but under the water curtain where the blind wall appeared to join the rock of the ravine, it didn't.

The blind wall was at a 45-degree angle to the ravine wall. Coming in on the rock ledge, you pass the point where you would see the opening because of the contour of the wall where the stone of the cataract would join the ravine wall. In such a restricted space it was completely invisible.

We squeezed through the opening, and found stairs going down, and stairs going up, convenient for a quick exit from either level. Our lights showed a tiny area at the bottom of the stairs, a landing perhaps, there was nothing there so we braved it and went down the stairs.

The mechanism was similar to the one the other side except it was a corner wall that jogged 3-feet in, and the wall continued on down the side of the chamber. This time the door swung out into the room, when closed no line was visible on the rock.

We almost got ourselves shot, and probably would have been if the chief hadn't been there to order them to hold their fire. Can you imagine the scare we got when the door opened and 6-guns were pointing at us?

The chief was angry that we would do a foolish thing as that without backup, but another step in securing this place was accomplished, and that mollified him somewhat. It didn't mollify Dad, however; he was angrier than Lexi had ever seen him he told me later.

"The chief showed me the video of that horror, were you going to take it on alone, unarmed, not telling anyone where you were going? If it cornered you in there you'd be finished, and we wouldn't know where the hell you were, I'm going to put leashes on both of you."

"One more stunt like that, and the police will know about the video, I understand why you want to keep it quiet, but I'm not going to risk losing either of you. Now, have I your word you won't disappear on a whim again?"

Two very contrite would be heroes nodded in unison. He was angry because he loves us, another new experience as part of a family.

Lexi started, "Dad, we're sorry we got you so upset, we found the stairs, there was nothing there, and our excitement got the upper hand over caution."

I interrupted him, "He's telling the truth Dad, we were totally horrified by that thing. If we had paused for a few seconds we wouldn't have gone down there alone, fools rush in, and we we're the fools. It won't happen again, promise."

He put his arms around us and hugged us tight, I think he was crying. I felt like an ass and Lexi did too.

When the furor died down the chief got three of his men and we went in the secret door again to see where the second set of stairs led us. From the stone shelf it was easy 100-feet to the top of the ravine that meant almost 200-steps.

I tried to imagine that creature tripping over itself trying to negotiate that many steps, he's not human; I told myself he most likely has more staying power than I have. We headed up the stairs, paused to show the chief how the exit was disguised by the blind wall, and started up the second-flight.

At about the tenth switchback the stairs ended, and a tunnel ran into what had to be the ravine wall. It ran straight ahead for maybe 60-feet, I figured we had already passed under the path going up the incline to the pasture land.

At the end of the tunnel the area opened width-wise, but the way ahead was restricted by a large mound of debris, from a partial cave-in. The debris wasn't too hard to get over, and on the other side was another cave, 10-feet-wide and 20-feet-deep, the mouth of the cave was plainly visible though shielded by thick bushes outside.

The way we came in, and the mouth of the cave were the only access points. We cautiously approached the entrance; even with the thicket in front of us we had an unrestricted view of the path in both directions.

No indication that wild animals had ever lived here, it seemed, no bones, no animal hair in the floor soil, and no scratch marks anywhere. Again Tomas was correct in his theory that animals will not go near this evil.

"If we can control all the entrances and exits, and have the swat team sweep through the tunnels and chambers with our security guys guarding the tunnel entrances," Lexi was strategizing with Dvorak and chief, "We could clear the cavern permanently."

"I don't like using civilians in a police operation," Dvorak complained, "But if it means we can wrap this smelly hole up and secure it, then I'm willing to bend the rules a little, which means you do no searching on your own. You just guard the entrances to the tunnels."

"That's okay with us," the chief said, "But if the little bugger your men already shot comes out, we fire."

"Okay, first thing tomorrow we do the sweep again, with the lights and breathable air it should be a piece of cake, but we don't take unnecessary chances, in our line of work it can get you dead."

The geologist approached me with a worried look; he had finished his tests for gas in the lower caverns and had some disturbing information to relay,

"The spectrometer showed a high concentration of ethylene gas in the lower level, it's mixed with high sulfur content, and an element the spectrometer couldn't identify, it would take a chromatograph to possibly identify it."

"Thousands of chemical compounds and combinations of them exist, the chromatograph will separate the most likely elements from the arcane, and give us an answer that's reliable."

"Do you think this unknown element in the gas can be causing the mutations we see in this creature?" I asked rather alarmed that we were all ingesting this gas.

"Gas will cause hallucinations, make you seriously ill, mess up your brain, and make you mentally incompetent, but it doesn't affect the physical until the mental deals with evolution, in other words it takes generations before the mental causes changes in the physical."

"I have several vials of the strongest concentrations registered on the spectrometer; a chemist familiar with toxicology may be able to enlighten us as to the unknown element."

Dad spent the rest of the afternoon talking to Tomas, analyzing different components of the story, much passed from previous generations, part of it experienced personally. Dad's main area of contention was the vampire legends, still believed today.

If this story were to go viral it would need some credibility, tales of vampires having orgies in remote mountain castles makes good fiction, but not believed to ever have been fact. To dispel the notion that what we have here is just the superstitious beliefs of people caught in a time warp, we have to make it believable.

"Tomas," Dad began, "Your ancestors passed on stories of vampires running rampant in the mountain villages, and they went from here to other locations in European cities, where did all these vampires come from?"

"If a vampire attacks and doesn't drain the victim so he or she dies, the victim only needs to drink a few drops of the attackers blood, if he were created by Vlad, to become a vampire also." Tomas replied,

"This was part of the knowledge the Hunters gave our forefathers so we knew what we were fighting. Vampires are immortal, the mortals die-off, but the vampires keep increasing in numbers year after year, until they outnumber the local population of mortals."

"The villages were just breeding places for their meals. When they became too numerous, and the small population couldn't support so many, they began to leave to replace the vampires being killed by the Hunters in the cities. Vlad had dreams of conquest and revenge on Romania, and the Hunters."

Dad thought for a minute, he didn't want Tomas to think he was challenging his account of the past,

"Why is the village not overrun by vampires again? It's been more than 300-years since the Hunters rid you of that scourge, and it's common belief that Vlad survived. Why wouldn't he create more vampires as he did before?"

"That is a question we ask ourselves constantly, and give thanks it has not happened. We speculate often on that subject, some make sense, some is fantasy; one major fantasy theory is the reason for the robes with the devil's marks."

"Satan was supposedly furious that Vlad had not vanquished the Hunters with all the powers he had bestowed on him; he took away his power to make more vampires as punishment and recruited mortals as his henchmen rather than vampires."

"Vlad was still their master, so the legend of the Satanists was started, and continued to day by bullies like the five in the cavern and the constable. Certain nights of the year, a fire would start in someone's house or barn, sometimes just a hay stack. Figures in white robes with the devil's markings, could be seen dancing around in front of the fire, to *be* seen obviously, and scare the villagers out of their wits."

"That's pretty hard to accept, what is there up here in the mountains that would attract the devil's attention and involvement?"

"I have put up an argument basically the same, why would Satan bother with a few remote mountain villages? It has always been ignored."

"What explanation makes sense?"

"The Hunters used silver to combat the vampires; it didn't kill them it just burned them badly, more importantly; it immobilized them so they could be staked or beheaded."

"The theory I agree with is that Vlad was caught in one of the Hunter's traps, and managed to escape, but was so badly burned that he couldn't create more vampires. With all the rest having fled, or been killed, the line was ended, but for Vlad."

"We found no trace of Vlad in the caverns, something is there, part animal part man, it was shot twice and didn't fall. Where do you think Vlad could be hiding out?"

"The villagers that worked on Vlad's castle reported large underground cellars and dungeons, when the castle was destroyed, the walls were collapsed into the cellars, and there could be subterranean caves still accessible."

"That would mean another cave to clean up," Dad sighed, "If we're to put an end to this, it will have to be done."

Another night of abstinence, if our mission for these people weren't so important we would leave for home in an instant. We sat in the barroom discussing the video of Tomas, and how best to present it. Dad found him a credible witness, high praise coming from a man who looks for credibility in a hundred ways, inflection, hesitation, nervousness, eye movement, and body language being a few. He can 'read' people effortlessly, and they are completely unaware he is doing it.

When Lexi was a kid, he told me, his father would 'read' his friends and tell them he knew what they were up to. His friends all thought Dad was a mind reader, and were scared to death of him.

We talked of ways to present questions not to be leading or combative, remaining neutral, but sympathetic was a challenge, with anyone other than Lexi that is. I've watched him since New Years, and he can talk the birds down from the trees, his manner, and empathy make him an easygoing interrogator. As I've said before, not one person he asked questions of, ever refused to cooperate.

The timing of the video was an issue, should we videotape the interview, send a feature story about it to NY first, have it translated with subtitles, or dub in the foreign languages? All choices were going to take time.

We agreed it had to wait until the cavern was secured, and the power station a reality; otherwise it might appear a publicity ploy to garner support. As soon as the police pronounced the area secure; we'd do the video.

Meanwhile, Tomas had to keep an ear out for changes in attitude of any village man. To date he had no indication from any villager of a change, which may mean they went over to the dark side by mind power of the master. Better to be vigilant than to be surprised.

Back to the cavern early Friday morning, we assumed it would all be over today, and we could have the weekend at home, it was just beginning.

The police fanned out to assault the tunnels again, the chief stationed his men one in front of each tunnel entrance. The geologist and his crew had left the previous afternoon, that left Dad, the chief, Lexi, and me, we gathered at the center of the room to view the video recordings of the night before if any.

The creature was caught on tape again, a little less furtive than before, and wasn't as concerned in tearing down the motion operated light as fast. We had a few more second of viewing before the screen went black. We hadn't succeeded in scaring him away, the threat remained, where did it go during the day?

A shot, and running feet, immediately at attention the guards had weapons in hand and safeties off, the bright lights in the tunnels let us see the thing before it exited the tunnel, not knowing there was a reception committee waiting for it. The guard in front of that tunnel entrance gasped and didn't hesitate, firing two silver tipped bullets into its chest.

It stopped in its tracks, looked down at its chest, then pitched forward on its face, the chief went closer to it, and fired another round into the back of its head. Not a twitch. Dead. Sgt. Dvorak came running, he turned to the body, and with his foot rolled the thing over, and vomited on the floor. The chief, always thinking took a picture of the thing with the sergeant standing over it puking.

The other police came running into the chamber, those who didn't vomit were gagging, and it had the same reaction with the security guards. It wasn't just the repulsive look of the thing it was the stench, it stank of rotting flesh, a gag reflex was a completely normal reaction.

I moved as far from it as I could get with Lexi moving beside me. We were almost at the stairs when a screeching began in the tunnel, and we glimpsed another of the things moving away from the central chamber.

The police, still retching, were thrown off guard by the horror lying on the floor. I noticed that the security lights had come on so the cameras would tell us where it had gone. The camera at the foot of the stairs was running, meaning we probably had the whole disgusting scene on video.

It took a couple of minutes for everyone to regain his composure, and the police went into action again, back into the tunnels with murder on their minds, their stances were fueled by vengeance on nature for allowing these demons from hell to exist.

The morning passed into afternoon, and no sign of the twin horror was found. The security cameras were not that deep in the tunnels, and he was out of sight if not sound, the screeching lasted for minutes, and echoed in the tunnels, so there was no direction that could be pinpointed.

Sergeant Dvorak called Olomouc and arranged for a helicopter to pick up the corpse as soon as possible, we didn't want to be saddled with that overnight. An ETA of a half-hour was one we could live with, and we waited to see it removed.

A plastic container was requested that could be sealed for the sake of the pilot's stomach. When the chopper arrived we quickly loaded it into the container, and were grateful to be rid of it.

CHAPTER 15

UNDER THE CASTLE

Nobody prepared to leave, it was a given that the work here was not done, so we gave Tomas the good news that he had a full house again, possibly for a few more days.

Dad called a disappointed Mom, she hadn't been here to see this creature, it didn't matter how much of a horror it was. Foremost to her as a medical doctor was the curiosity of its existence, its physiognomy, and I'd wager she wouldn't even gag. Dad sent a picture of it he had taken on his cell phone; she gave a little gasp and said,

"So this is what a demon from hell looks like, you men have all the fun. Take care of my boys and stay away from creatures like this, they wouldn't make good pets."

Mom can be a comic, and laugh in life's face until someone needs help, then she's all business. Lexi gets his empathetic qualities from her; she's quite a woman to have in your corner.

Contemplative, morose, shaken, and freaked out are some descriptive words for the patrons of the inn's barroom Friday night, police and civilians alike. Maybe I should have included shock, several police, and security guards were not prepared for such a confrontation, their blank stares told us as much.

Dad was worried they wouldn't admit psychological problems caused by the sudden exposure to inexplicable horror. We at least were forewarned, whether we were believers or not, when the horror appeared we had some knowledge of the possibilities.

Dad spoke in a quiet voice, "Now I can more clearly see the terror Tomas was trying to show us, it's so far out in left field we can't believe. It sounded exaggerated, if anything Tomas was very conservative, after what we saw today."

"The problem we have is how to present such horror to the public without causing panic. The answer is the same as the government would devise, we can't. I don't think we will ever discover what the genealogy of the creature was; it will never come to light."

"We still have victims who deserve redress, how do we achieve that without letting the foul air out of the balloon? Boys, we must be very careful with this video we're going to make, it could backfire and do more harm than good."

"You're going to be there all the way Dad," Lexi assured him, "You're going to edit every word of that video. You know more about what makes people do what they do than anyone I have ever even heard of. We're all together in this, we want the same thing for these people, and we're not going to do harm."

It even works on his father, I thought, Dads demeanor softened, and he relaxed a bit, leaning on his son's confident assurance that all would be well. What a guy.

Sergeant Dvorak came to our table and politely asked permission to sit with us. Surprised as we were, we tried not to show it, and graciously offered him a seat. I had a niggling feeling what was coming, but stayed silent so my diplomat could handle it.

"This incident today is a serious problem for the government. Are you aware of the panic in 1858 when it was reported that 2-vampires were captured feeding on their victims? Prague citizens went berserk; graves were dug up, corpses desecrated. Everybody accused his neighbor with whom they had the pettiest of disputes, of being a vampire. Hundreds died, the government could do nothing, it took on a life of its own."

"I only tell you this to mitigate the damage the truth of what is here will cause. I will pledge to you, and to these people we will remove this evil from their villages, I will petition the Ministry of Justice with all of you present to confirm what occurred here today."

"I know you have videos of the most evil entity I have ever encountered. I'm not going to confiscate them to show my good faith that you will help us finish this job without a public spectacle."

Damn, this sounds like Lexi, are all Czechs so persuasive. He convinced me with his argument, and I was ready to work with the government.

My diplomat wasn't so sure, "The government has a very poor record of openness even to other agencies of the same regime, by what authority do you make these promises."

"May I call you Lexi," he asked, "I have heard others call you that. I want you to believe I'm sincere, not the government, but me. You have the videotapes, Lexi, and if I don't come through as I promise you can release them in any manner you wish. If you release them it will most likely be the end of my career with the Federal Police, but after today I'm not sure I can deal with everything that's happened."

Dad was thoughtfully tapping his fingers on the table, and said. "What you are feeling is not as unusual as you may think. Many strong, good men when they see the horror of war, for example, wanton killing, or bloody massacres, it makes them ill, in the sense that it goes against their moral convictions. It's not a physical sickness, you will slowly recover from this shock; I hope the rest of the men do too."

"What have you planned for tomorrow? I think it would be advisable to stay away from the cavern for a day and let your mind accept what we saw."

"Sergeant, why don't we check out the ruins of the castle?" Lexi suggested, "Tomas tells us there may be hiding places around there still, we at least will get an idea of what's possible."

"A break from the horror of that cavern would be appreciated by all," he agreed, "We'll do that first thing in the morning."

We said good-night to everyone, and went to our room, to hold each other through the night hoping to make the fear and anxiety go away, I'm not sure I could have made it without Lexi, it was the worst night I had ever spent, nothing my father had ever done came close to this.

In the morning Lexi told me of his sleeplessness and reruns of the day's events, he said he was glad I was there to ease the anguish. I guess between us we managed to diminish our fear and give each other comfort.

Vlad's castle sat on a high promontory overlooking the river and the falls; you would miss it completely if you weren't given directions. Tomas explained why the signs the government had erected, disappeared.

The castle had been an object of fear and hatred for 3-centuries. No matter whether the much-needed tourist dollars poured in or not, each time the signs were erected again, they would disappear the next day. The local populace was not proud of the landmark in their midst.

We found the road thanks to the directions Tomas had provided, even in late spring the road was a challenge, I couldn't imagine trying to get up there in winter without a snowmobile. The castle wasn't as well defended as I thought it would be, the approach up the mountain road went directly to what was the outer wall. A rotting iron porte-cullis imbeded in the dirt told the tale, the peasants attacking the castle had dismantled the few safety features Vlad had bothered with. Being remote and inaccessible by any large force, he would know well in advance of an armed group approaching his castle.

Popular fiction has the villagers with torches, and pitchforks attacking the castle, but according to our local historian, Tomas, the villagers attacked in daylight, they knew it would be foolhardy to attack when the vampires were the strongest.

With help from the peasants Vlad had pressed into serving him, the porte-cullis opened, the mob took control of the castle and dismantled it.

Vampires not staked through the heart, escaped through hidden passages, and found later as the demolition progressed, it took weeks, and vampires were found each day hiding in cellars, or cowering in their coffins. They were summarily staked and dragged out to the sunlight to be destroyed.

There wasn't much left to look at; a rock foundation on a fifty-acre plateau, with walls still a few inches above the ground. Several areas around the considerable perimeter were higher, from one foot to several feet, but it was a total ruin. The rock floors were mostly intact, and a stairway down to the cellars was evident at the rear of the castle's footprint.

Access to the cellars wasn't restricted, but there was nothing at the bottom of the stairs but rubble, they collapsed the walls of the castle into the cellars. We did the tourist thing, and saw every attraction pointed out by signs, nothing convincing here.

We did a perimeter check, and found this castle had a first-floor area of more than 17,000-square-feet, how many floors did this place have? Three? Four? More? It could have accommodated hundreds of vampires, the place had been huge. A new respect for folk lore and legend found its way into our thinking.

The chief suggested we look in the woods near the ruins, a stroll to grammas house through the dark forested area surrounding a much-maligned piece of real estate.

The castle was built at the highest point on the promontory, so any exits would have to be down the precipice. We found no indications of paths or ledges that would indicate an escape route, when I thought about what I was looking at, it stuck me that the Hunters must have viewed the same terrain and arrived at the same conclusion.

Was there a difference they hadn't noticed? I couldn't find one, why were the villagers so certain that there were still areas under the ruins, a refuge for monsters? The answer came from history as in our innkeeper, Tomas. Villagers built the castle; they labored for years under brutal oppression, every secret, every false wall, every hidden cavern was known to these unwilling laborers.

However many the monster Vlad had killed, the knowledge didn't die. The knowledge of the underground cellars survived from worker to worker, and to Tomas, who heard it from his father's, father's, father.

Word of mouth is largely discounted in our history of the world, would there even be a history without it? How can a people relate their experiences to posterity, if they don't have scribes, video cams, and voice recorders? These people had no such advantage, they told, and retold the stories handed down from generations before them, based on superstition or fact?

So far the score card is in favor of fact, everything Tomas has related to us has been, even if not proven, the solution to some of our problems, like silver bullets.

The part of the castle that faced the river was built on the edge of a vertical precipice; the wall of the castle was a continuation of the rock. Very thick for strength, and proved somewhat impervious to the villagers destructive blows, much of that wall was standing sentinel over the ruins below, that wall alone was impressive, the castle must have been a sight to behold.

The base of the escarpment was 70-feet from the plateau and piled high with rock debris, nothing to indicate a means to enter a subterranean cave system. One reason for the belief that a cave existed beneath the castle was the fact that this whole area of the mountains was riddled with caves. Sonic testing wouldn't help, the collapsed walls undoubtedly had large voids that would look like caves, but were inaccessible.

The sergeant and the chief left the plateau to survey the surrounding forest, and below the escarpment. We were about to leave when Lexi climbed on the wall, to get a better view of the ravine and falls.

Heights leave my knees weak, and my head spinning, but it was Lexi up on the wall, and still vertigo claimed me as the victim, I was seeing the dizzying drop through his eyes. That's something new, was I in his mind with him?

"Get down here Lexi, you're going to go over the edge, you have no idea if that wall is stable, it could collapse, and take you with it." I pointlessly argued.

He turned to me, and gave me his smile that conceals a thousand messages. Ignoring my pleas, he turned back to the view, which I'm sure was spectacular. He suddenly became interested in something in the forest below; he jumped down, much to my relief, and grabbing my arm pulled me along the path that the chief had taken.

"We have to catch up with them," he said, "There's a line in the forest, I saw it from up on the wall, there's no other vantage point where you can see it, I think it's a trail from the river to the forest west of the escarpment, it could lead us to Vlad's hiding place."

We caught up with them moments later, Lexi excitedly explained what he had seen, "It's just a little way to the east, it won't hurt to check it out."

"That's a welcome development," the chief replied, "We've struck out here so far, lead on; I hope it's not just a game trail."

We found the trail where Lexi had indicated, it was much more traveled than a normal game trail would be unless it led to water. No streams or ponds were nearby, so it must have regular travelers with a specific destination in mind.

Following the trail, we estimated we were about 100-feet below the level of the plateau when it ended at the mouth of a cave. Because there was no attempt to conceal it, we considered it just a cave, a den for a mother bear and her cubs, explaining the trail.

"Have you ever read 'The Purloined Letter'?" Sgt. Dvorak asked to no one in particular, "Hiding something in plain sight is a diabolically clever ploy, we're ready to dismiss it as nothing more than it appears to be, a cave, a den."

"Let's have a look then, and put it to rest," the chief remarked querulously, "We have to approach cautiously in case an animal is in there."

With that warning voiced, he moved forward with hesitant steps to peer into the cave, it was unoccupied. We had the small helmet lights with us, and it illuminated the small space enough to tell it was deeper than we thought; through a narrow opening we could see the cave extended back beyond the range of our lights.

"Bingo," I exclaimed, "It pays to read even Poe, this has to be the cave system the villagers refer to, it's close enough to the ruins, about the same level where the dungeons would be and it stinks of something I'd rather forget."

As dignified as we could, we backed out of the cave considering the panic we were feeling. Backup was imperative before entering here.

Still early Saturday morning, we raced back to the inn; the sergeant went to round up his men, chief to round up his. We found Dad talking to Tomas, Lexi explained the cave's location so Tomas could give us any insight he had, but he had no idea of a cave at that location.

The cave had avoided detection for 3-centuries because all mountain people shunned the general area, and outsiders hunting game or mountain-climbing would think what the chief had suggested, an animal's den to be avoided.

"You had better take a can of spray paint; Tomas tells me the caves below the castle are supposedly vast, and very confusing. He presumes that's the reason the mob and the Hunters didn't venture down there to find Vlad.

Rumor had it there was no way out, so they dropped the walls into the cellars to block anyone from going in or trying to come out. If this cave is an entrance, you'll have to mark your progress."

I could tell Dad wanted to come with us, and was waiting for an invitation.

Before Lexi could put the brakes on the idea I said,

"Why don't you come with us and be our map maker, seeing as it was your idea?"

Lexi growled at me but held his peace; to refuse his father would be reversing their roles.

"We stay in the rear I think the men out front should mark our passage. If the police split up, they should use different colors, at least we'll know where they went if they don't show up at the appointed time. Let's make that suggestion to Dvorak."

Apparently Dvorak was way ahead of us, "In the event we have to split up there's going to be a time limit of one hour, and by then be back at the starting point. That means going forward for only one-half-hour.

Five teams of four men with separate colors, our communication gear probably won't work in there, but we'll try to stay in touch as long as we can, if there's trouble be careful, if you have to fire your weapon a stray bullet could bring a ton of ceiling down on your head. Shoot at the head if you see the other creature, decapitate if possible."

Back to the castle, unhappy campers, yesterday's horror still front and center in all our minds, and now another cave to assault. I wondered how many of these men would stay with their service after this ordeal.

We had sandwiches on our way to the cave and I made a furtive plea to allow us to keep the food down. Entering the cave, and with better lighting, saw the labyrinth we were walking into.

Passages going everywhere, the sergeant gave his instructions, they were to take five passages all going roughly toward the castle, trying to stay in that line, going back to check if necessary. Spray painting at 50-foot intervals in conspicuous locations to not get turned around. Then he said,

"This is just a preliminary look see to gauge what we're up against. One-half-hour should be enough time to observe how complicated the operation is. Be careful."

One-hour later the police started filing from the passages, all accounted for and noticeably shaken, they found skeletons and parts of skeletons in huge numbers. Lost with no food or water was the probable cause of death, more than a few had fangs, escapees from the Hunters no doubt.

No central area was found, possibly farther in toward the castle. They had kept count of the fifty-foot intervals and computed the approximate distance traveled, they had gone an average of a little more than a half-mile that wasn't far enough to be under the castle; that had to be more than a mile away.

The effort wasn't wasted, we now had a path, five actually, to follow, it would be faster the next foray into the labyrinth.

At the inn, Sergeant Dvorak announced to us, "I'm calling the Justice Minister in a few minutes, so you know what I'm up to, I'm requesting a crew of professional cave explorers, and cartographers to help us, we can't possibly secure this maze, its beyond our capabilities."

"My men and I will stay on to offer some protection to the explorers. I'll report to you when I finish talking to the Minister."

Ten-minutes and he was back,

"I have some bad news, the Justice Minister and the Prime Minister want to talk to us on Sunday at 9:00 a.m. that means you guys, my crew, and me. I made a point of asking exactly to whom he wanted to speak, he wants everybody involved. He said there are some startling developments that he couldn't relate over an unsecure line."

"A helicopter, probably two, will be here at 8:00 a.m., it's only a 30-minute flight, they're in Olomouc now, this is strange, I have a bad feeling about this."

"Aren't they normally in Prague?" Dad asked, "What would take them to Olomouc on a weekend?"

"We'll discover that tomorrow at 9:00 a.m.," Dvorak answered, "It's very unusual for the two highest-ranking officials to be involved in a district matter at the same time."

CHAPTER 16

INTERVIEW WITH TOMAS & THE PM

We had dinner with Tomas to go over the dialogue for the video, but the conversation was speculation about tomorrow. We were all thinking basically the same scenario, an extremely concerned government worried that news of these creatures would become public information, and we need a large broom to sweep it under the rug, the same old story.

Another troubled night, it seemed to never end, the hours dragged on so slowly, while sleep was elusive, nightmares were the main pictures moving through my brain when sleep visited for a brief period.

Morning did arrive, so did the helicopters, two large troop carriers set down in the village square, right outside of our room. The villagers were terrified, more from the noise than from fear of invasion; they got over it fast enough to have a close-up look at these flying marvels before they took off.

At 8:30 a.m. we set down in Olomouc, near the county seat, two of the Prime Minister's representatives greeted us and led us into the government building eerily silent on a Sunday morning. A breakfast buffet was set up with every sort of breakfast food you could imagine. Coffee was the best, not strong and bitter, like most coffee served in Europe, this reminded me of NY.

I relaxed somewhat, and ate a little, the appetite was missing; the smell of the creature was still in my nostrils. Lexi had no such problem he dug in like a starving man rescued from a desert island.

The Prime Minister, the Justice Minister, their aids, and a dozen other officials joined us and we were introduced. The caterers cleared the remains of the breakfast, and left.

The PM, a very gracious man, possibly an aristocrat with impeccable manners, asked us to sit, and dropped a bomb in our newly created laps.

"Gentlemen, we have a problem, the creature that you had shipped back here on Friday afternoon was not dead," We started to talk, all at the same time, "Let me finish, when the coroner accepted the cadaver, he claims it was dead, I'm sure all of you will claim the same thing; however, on Saturday two young medical interns were preparing for the autopsy."

"Everything done during an autopsy, is videotaped, it was running, what we witnessed on that tape cannot be put into words. I know you were subjected to the real thing, so I won't put you through the gruesome details. When they opened the drawer that thing leapt on the young man and ripped out his throat."

"The young woman was frozen in horror, the creature turned to her and was more leisurely with her, he sucked every drop of blood from her body, threw her aside, and drained the male. I'm not going to give anymore details, they're too ghoulish."

"Both bodies are in the morgue as we speak. It tried to leave the locked autopsy room; all our lab doors lock automatically. Frustrated, it started howling, or screeching, I don't know what it was, but it was heard by many medical personnel in the building at the time that went to see what the racket was all about."

"A few saw the thing rip the door off the autopsy room, wisely they disappeared before it spotted them, they reported it found the stairs up to the first floor and ran out the main entrance. The second it was outside of the building it began screeching again, and disappeared down the street at an incredible speed. Now I want to hear some details from you, what is that thing?"

Sgt. Dvorak stood and identified himself as the lead investigating officer at the scene,

"I sent my men into the tunnels under the main cavern to clear out any more assassins. We found a partially decomposed body of an adult male that put my men on high alert."

"In a different chamber, something was hiding behind a pile of bones. Thinking it was a man, we ordered it to come out, what we saw was that creature, it ran, and was shot twice, it didn't stop. The next time we did the sweep with the men ready to end the horror, again it was shot, and again, it didn't stop."

"It ran out into the central chamber where the security guards, hired by the foundation backing the power station, were facing the tunnel entrances with their weapons at the ready. They shot it twice in the chest, it fell, the chief of the security guards went to the body, and shot it in the head, point blank, I witnessed that shot myself."

"If that didn't kill it, then there's nothing that can. Alexi Duburk is a partner in the foundation for the power plant; he can explain how their bullets stopped it when our larger caliber rounds could not."

I crossed my fingers, Lexi convince them, he started,

"Mr. Prime Minister, thank you for the chance to explain our mission, and our quest to alleviate the suffering of the mountain people, our fellow citizens. What I am about to tell you is going to be met with incredulity, but with the tapes you have seen yourself maybe it won't be so incredulous."

"The people of the village in question are very open and welcoming, we talked to many of them and all endorsed economic development, my partner, Carl Wellsey is an American, together we set up the foundation the sergeant referred to. It's a nonprofit, any funds generated–no pun intended, over operating costs will go to economic development for the communities."

"When we tried to get information from the villagers about the survey done 25 or 30-years ago, no one would talk about it but to say the waterfall was an evil place. We didn't push them, they are very reticent people, and we tried to respect their privacy."

"They invited us to their May Day celebrations, which confirmed their attitude of hospitality and welcoming to all, an uplifting experience. We had, for me anyway, the best time I've ever had at a May Day celebration, Carl thoroughly enjoyed it too."

"The next morning we were walking along the river when Carl saw a woman push a child into the freezing river, without a moment's hesitation, he went into the river to save the child. He got her by the hair and pulled her to him, and tried to get them out of the river. With the help of the innkeeper Tomas, we managed to extend a tree branch for Carl to hold onto."

"When we finally pulled them from river, both were suffering from hypothermia, luckily, they survived, and the outcome was that Carl was now a local hero. Their outlook on life is pretty simple 'you risk your life for one of ours, then you are one of us', Carl eschews the title of hero, he only did what any thinking person would do."

"It had an unexpected result, they opened up to us, as if they owed us something, they related the most incredible story any person in my generation has ever heard."

"You must know of the ruins of Vlad the Impaler's castle in those mountains, its part of our history and folklore, but it's not fiction. The castle existed, Vlad existed he was a Romanian King. The legends fade our understanding of the horror these people have endured for centuries."

"Our security chief checked reports for more than 20-years of crimes, and unexplained incidents in this valley. The reports are sorted by village, chronologically, and by severity of the crime. Your honor, I am a loyal subject of the Czech Republic, I was incensed that for so long these people have been ignored, their issues denigrated to insignificance."

"Tomas, the inn keeper lost his son, in the middle of winter when they are isolated as they had been for generations. In the spring the village constable declared him a runaway. Dozens of these reports were obtained from a tiny mountain valley with 3,000-occupants at best."

"The crime rate in this bucolic paradise is more than twice the crime rate per capita in Prague. The saying goes 'the squeakiest wheel gets the grease', the complaints of the villagers fell on deaf ears, they weren't squeaking loudly enough. Ignoring them is disgusting behavior from a government who claims to be the champion of all the people."

"We have a videotape of the innkeeper telling his story, leading up to the present, it's all word of mouth, from one generation to the next, should we discount it? Is truth telling reserved for the powerful in Prague? Tomas told us of the Hunters—vampire killers, who came to their village because it was a birthing point for new vampires."

"Vlad the Impaler was a prince of the Draculesti court; he was a ranking prince, he had enormous power, friend and foe alike feared him. He fled to this area because he was betrayed by a son or brother who wanted his kingdom."

"It's history, we have the ruins of his castle, we have found extensive caves under his castle, when do we stop thinking its all superstition and legend? I'll tell you when, watch the videotape again and there will be no question."

"Vampires are real. Do not discount these people who have suffered for so long, this creature is some mutated version of a vampire, but does it matter? It's as lethal as anything that your arsenal can handle."

"One last point, Tomas related the Hunters explanation for using silver against the vampires, he said silver immobilizes them, burns them badly, but doesn't kill them. We shot this creature with silver tipped

Charles Walker

bullets, twice through the heart, and one directly into its brain, how could any creature survive that? Its power of regeneration must be phenomenal."

"Again according to the Hunters, there are three ways to kill a vampire; exposure to sunlight, a wooden stake in the heart and decapitation. These creatures must be mutations, if it ran out into the sunlight and didn't perish immediately; the screaming indicates the light was having some negative effect on it."

The PM responded with a question, "You said creatures, how numerous are they?"

"Only two that we know of, there was no indication of multiple residences, the bedding we found was for two. I think if there were more of them the killings in the village and farms would be far worse."

"We still don't know if the one the assassins called the 'master' is Vlad, or where he could be hiding during the daytime. Sergeant Dvorak can tell you about the caves beneath the castle ruins. Thank you for listening to us."

The PM was a study of worry and chagrin simultaneously, "I would like to hear what our Minister of Justice thinks of all this."

"I, too have seen the morgue video; if it weren't for that I wouldn't even be discussing the existence of vampires. Your presentation young man was excellent, if you weren't so young I'd think you a seasoned Politian."

"You seem to know volumes more than we do about vampires. Mr. Prime Minister I would like to recruit these young men to work with us to clear up this mess."

"I agree, would you be willing to help us rid the world of this scourge? Both of you can be invaluable in getting things done that would take a bureaucrat months to accomplish. I noticed in your speech your disdain for government, please don't think us a group of uncaring, and unfeeling politicians."

"As much as we would like to take action, there is opposition to every suggestion made by either side; politics is, in the end, the art of

188

compromise. If we sent a battalion to the mountains without approval from both sides, we would be accused of all sorts of mischief, if we brought the issue to the floor for debate we would have to show the morgue video, what would do in my position? Show the video?"

Lexi stood, "Mr. Prime Minister, I won't presume to give advice to you, but no, I wouldn't release the video, it would be all over the media in hours. As for sending troops to these mountains, we can give you the report on criminal activity there, with no mention of vampires. Believe me sir the report is alarming; anyone with a social conscience will be appalled at such a high crime rate with a relatively small population. If I may ask, what is being done to find the creature?"

"Are you with us?"

Lexi looked at me for confirmation, but he knew me well enough that I would do it, perhaps he didn't want them to think he was arrogantly speaking for both of us. I nodded, he said, "Yes"

"Then I'm not giving up state secrets. We have another swat team such as we sent to the mountains, they are working 24-hours a day, not a sign of the creature, no bodies drained of blood, and no reported sightings of a creature that would give people nightmares if they saw it. Do you have a theory where it might be?"

"I'm guessing now, but logically he would go to ground, they may have some immunity from sunlight, but why would it start screeching when it got outside if it were fully immune? My best guess is it's hiding somewhere dark during the day, possibly healing itself, regaining its strength. It's too much to hope that the sun did it in."

Lexi did it again, they we eating it up as if he were an expert on the subject, my boy had the gift.

"Good thinking, we've been treating it as a wild animal; maybe it didn't go very far at all, and is hiding very close to us." The Justice Minister observed, "Another sweep through this area might flush it out."

We spent two more hours explaining the cave system, and what we needed to deal with its complexities. The Prime Minister directed the head of justice to give the swat team everything it needed, cave explorers, and map makers being the most urgent necessity of the operation.

A helicopter took the chief, Lexi, and me back to the mountains with the chief beaming at us as if we were kids bringing home a good report card,

"You two are a hell of a team, I got a feeling we're going to be hearing a lot more from you in the future."

"Thanks chief but you're forgetting the boost you gave us on this fracas," Lexi stated, "Your strategy is what brought us this far."

Lexi wasn't snowing the chief, he's a valuable part of our group no one, or two, of us can do this thing without the help of the others, and we wanted him to stay with us.

Dad was waiting for us at the band shell to avoid the wind from the rotors, we related the events of the day, and he as stunned,

"There's not a creature alive that can recover from a shot in the brain, did you see the video?"

"No," Lexi said, "We didn't want to pile on more nightmares. The PM doesn't want anyone else to see it; he fears a leak, and the ensuing media circus. He wants us to work with them to end this; I don't think it was to keep us quiet; he's a sophisticated man who saw a heinous act committed on camera. He needs all the help he can get."

"There's another aspect to this," I said, "If we co-operate with the government to get rid of this problem, we will have a much easier time of it when we start work on the power station. We need permits, road improvements, reinforcing the bridge, land grants, inspections, and a hundred other little things that bedevil contractors under the thumb of the government."

"Whose little brain is running full speed now?" Lexi quipped, "I only wanted to help them for altruistic reasons."

"Lexi that's a crock and you know it," Dad shot back, "It isn't wrong to expect a favor for a favor unless it's a criminal conspiracy."

"I didn't mean it that way Dad, the farthest thing from my mind is Carl doing something illegal, he knows I'm teasing. Do you think I didn't consider the advantage of working for the government when we were asked by the Prime Minister himself? Carl saw me give him a look when the offer was made; I knew we were thinking alike when he gave a little nod."

"I should stay out of your banter, sometimes it sounds as if you're angry, this time I thought you were putting him down." Dad said apologetically.

"I have only been angry with Carl once; the first day we met. As to me putting him down, I wouldn't do that for any reason. I love him, why would I denigrate him?"

"Family Feud episode one, take two," I joked, "As the butt of this dustup, let me say, 'I am not a crook', we're a team Dad, in each other's pocket always, don't fret over little barbs we throw at each other, it's all in fun."

"Seriously folks, can we do the video with Tomas today, we told the PM that we had the video already, I was worried he would ask to see it. He probably had enough videos for one day, but he's going to want to see it eventually."

"Let's go ask him," Dad said, "I just left him when I heard the chopper. He seems pretty chipper, so I don't think it's a good idea to tell him about the creature right away,"

"Tomas we're going to make you a movie star," Lexi teased, "Make up? No? Okay, we'll go au naturel. Where do you want to video this, in front of the fireplace? Behind the bar?"

"I'll feel more comfortable behind the bar," Tomas said, "Maybe I should have a beer or two so I won't be nervous."

"Not a good idea Tomas, you have to alert and articulate if this video is going to work." Dad added.

"Carl would you handle the camera? Dad is going to follow the script so we don't leave anything out. Let's get started."

"Good afternoon Mr. Danik, My name is Alexi Duburk, I would like to ask you some question about this village."

"Good afternoon Mr. Duburk, I am ready to answer to the best of my ability."

"What is your position here in the village?"

"I am the inn keeper."

"Do you have any influence with the people as inn keeper?"

"If I do it's because I try to be fair, and treat all in the same manner."

"Why did you agree to do this interview?"

"We are tired of the government ignoring our pleas for justice, tired of the way we are thought of by our fellow citizens of the Czech Republic, and tired of living in these conditions."

"What conditions do you refer to?"

"The fear we live in, our family members going missing, farm animals mutilated, family pets slaughtered, and threats of reprisals from our constable if we criticize his performance."

"We are prisoners, we have been for generations, no one will help, no one will even listen. Late last October a young man brought his new wife to meet his grandparents, they never arrived. Two villagers hunting deer, found their bodies in November."

"The bodies were in the same condition as the mutilated farm animals, drained of blood, and throats ripped open. The one difference was that the young couple were brutally sexually assaulted. The woman's vagina was torn by something sadistically inserted in her, the man's anus was in the same condition, and his genitals were missing.

The authorities took the bodies for autopsy, we have heard nothing since."

"At the time we were told they had died of exposure, and the wound marks on the bodies were probably caused by wolves or bears. But, like the farm animals, in every instance slime is on the carcasses, wolves, and bears won't go near it. The same slime was on the couple. An evil force is working here."

"Can you tell us what the evil force is?"

"We only have rumors, superstition, legend, and speculation."

"Why should we believe in these legends and superstitions?"

"I lost my 14-year-old son 10-years ago; everyone in this village has lost someone, to what? Where have they gone? We are totally isolated here in the winter, no way in, and no way out. Where did a young boy go in subzero weather? These are stories the government doesn't want to hear. In the spring he was declared a runaway, runaway to where? How?"

"Do you know the pain of not knowing whether he was sexually assaulted like the young couple? Do you know the tears cried for loving your only child and being told he ran away from your family's love? What should we believe Mr. Duburk, what the government tells us or what we experience year in, and year out? Not in just my generation but in the recollections of my father and his father, it hasn't changed."

"Political systems change, Nazis, Communists, Tito, and now the European Union, it is still the same terror in our lives. Last week a study group came to our mountain village to determine the feasibility of a hydroelectric plant on our waterfall."

"That would start an economic boom so badly needed in this area. They were ambushed by bullies from our village. We are not against progress, the entire village supported this project, or so we thought. It seems the constable, and a few beholden to another master set out to stop the new effort in its tracks."

"Why would the constable and the 'bullies' as you call them, want to stop progress in an area so needing economic expansion?"

"The evil one's base is the cavern behind the falls. That area has been shunned by all for centuries. The evil one controls any mind coming into his area of influence, and he will protect his Domain, I understand that the police who went into the cavern found no sign of Vlad."

"What can be done to alleviate this problem?"

"The 'Hunters rid us of the scourge of vampires 300-years ago, they never found Vlad. Our belief is, he survived the purge, maybe with diminished powers, but his evil is still here, to get rid of it will take much courage, and a mind as cunning as his."

"Do you have any ideas where he may be?"

"The peasants forced to build his castle claimed it was built over a labyrinth of caves. When the people, with the Hunters help destroyed the castle, they collapsed the walls into the cellars, blocking access to any caves that might have been there. No other entrances have ever been found."

"Would you like this video to bring the government to help?"

"If it does that, we will be in your debt for all future generations Mr. Duburk"

"Thank you for agreeing to this interview Mr. Danik."

"Thank you for trying to help."

Lexi translated the interview into English, and I began to plan my story. The more I read, the more I admired him; he took a man who did not want to tell his troubles to anyone, and brought him around to telling it in a video in 3-weeks.

We took snap-shots of village people going about their business, and videos of the picturesque mountain scenery, the ruins of the castle, the waterfall, and pictures of the houses and barns with the strange shaped roofs.

This video and accompanying article was going to be a blockbuster.

CHAPTER 17

KILLING A HORROR FROM HELL

Lexi was the first to burst my bubble, "How are we going to release the video, we are working with the authorities, won't that be the same as leaking an official document?"

"I don't think our video has anything to do with the creature in Olomouc." I replied, "We told the PM we had the video of Tomas, maybe we should clear it with him, would that make you feel better?"

"I can't see any other avenue we have; the government will come down hard on us if we do it without their approval."

Lexi called the PM and actually got through to him, amazing, I still harbored doubts regarding their motive for asking us to be part of the team. He stayed on the line while Lexi e-mailed the video to him.

"I find the video very moving, and agree it would create much sympathy for the villagers." The PM said, "In the spirit of co-operation to solve this dilemma though, we should all be pulling in the same direction. It might inflame people, especially if the creature is not apprehended, and it becomes public knowledge because of another victim. The two issues are linked, and it may hurt your crusade more than it helps."

I couldn't fight the logic, he was right; the fact that it came from the valley would poison any sympathy felt initially.

Lexi massaged my neck as he said, "It'll still get published Carl, we have to wait until they capture, or kill the thing. We can't afford to make enemies of these men, they're very powerful, I'm not so sure they don't have the authority to order us not to publish it. Another outcome may be roadblocks put in our way for the power station, we can't jeopardize that."

Dinner was a dismal affair, not because of the food, but the depression that was covering the inn like Beijing smog, a vampire, or some mutation of one, outmaneuvered us. We needed a plan that would end this circus.

"Remember how the Hunters got many of the vampires, according to what Tomas told us?" I asked the assembly at the table, "They baited traps, using people as the bait." I waited for that to sink in; you could almost see the wheels in their heads turning. "Why shouldn't it work again?"

When the clamor died, Dad sounding stern said, "Don't even think of putting yourselves out there to be attacked by that God-awful horror,"

"We wouldn't be alone and unarmed, it's affected by silver, we saw that, if we protect the bait with silver and have the guards nearby with their silver bullets we should be safe. We can carry the silver nitrate aerosol containers, if it comes close enough, we aim for the eyes."

I stated as confidently as I could, because I didn't feel too confident. I had no wish to get close to that monster.

The chief had been thinking carefully during the uproar in response to my idea, he spoke up,

"We could make that work, and whoever the bait is would have to wear much silver under their clothing. Its hearing is nothing special, a force of 30-men went into the cavern, and it didn't try to escape until they were practically on top of it, and we weren't trying to be quiet."

"I think there should be 2-men as bait maybe, equipped with communication devices. I have a couple of sharpshooters in my squad, they'd be at the ready to take it down at the first opportunity, all our silver bullets are 9-millimeter so we need 9-millimeter rifles, maybe the police can furnish them to us."

Lexi, looking thoughtful, his mind racing added his opinion, "Two men might scare it off, how about two, but kept a good distance apart? If we can lure it out and the sniper can't get a clear shot, one of us sprays it with silver nitrate; the other comes up, and stakes it in the heart so it stays dead."

"How can we make this work here in the cavern?" I asked, "To do that in the tunnels would be suicide; there are too many places to be ambushed in there."

"The plan would only work in the open, and at night in Olomouc, here during the day it would work, but it would have to be flushed out, that's a problem. If it is coming after bait in the large chamber, the snipers would have to be hidden; it's not going to jump on the bait with 6-men pointing guns at it."

"Do you have a map of the tunnels?" the chief asked, "We'll have the police start their sweep on the opposite side of the cavern from the stairs, blocking it from using the exit there."

"They sweep in only four tunnels leaving the one closest to the stairs as his only means of retreat. That's the one where the other thing came out. With only 1-man visible from the tunnel, it will be confident it can attack and escape through the exit to the bridge, we hit it and stake it."

The police were due back in the morning. With plans made, and Dad not very happy, we left the barroom for the bedroom. In the room Lexi stripped off his clothes and said,

"I'm not waiting another night to have you in me, I've been wanting it for 3-days now, I don't care who hears us." As he was saying this he was helping me out of my clothes, "Let's take a bath we can play some water sports."

I was game for that, depression or revulsion wasn't going to stop the need I felt. We needed release from the crazy events that left us unsure what we wanted to do, we knew now, and we were going to do it. As the bathtub was filling, we kissed tenderly, rubbing our naked bodies together, feeling each other's face, and hair.

Only half full of hot-water, the tub threatening to overflow when we got in, some was drained off so we wouldn't flood the bathroom. It seemed so long since we had been intimate that we kept kissing and fondling each other until the water started to cool. We ran more hot-water, and went back to the work of making love.

I've never had sex in the back-seat of a car, it's supposedly very uncomfortable, that's the closest I can come to describing sex in a small bathtub. That's not a complaint; I would do it anywhere he wanted to.

We made it last until the water had no heat left, we climaxed together, dried each other, and fell happily asleep in each other's arms.

We called the police in Olomouc first thing Monday morning; they were still rounding up spelunkers and cartographers. We requested all the silver chains they could lay their hands on, and a couple of 9-millimeter rifles.

Scheduled to leave at noon, they had a few hours to search for chains; we suggested locating a wholesale jewelry supplier. The question that could not be answered by anyone living was how did the Hunters set traps, and use silver to immobilize the vampires?

Tomas could only speculate as we were doing, the chief's suggestion to wear silver under our clothes was reminiscent of a suit of armor, impractical. The final method of protection using silver was not wearing it at all, but using the chains as threads to weave a loose net to be thrown, or dropped over the vampire.

In the event there weren't enough chains to make a mesh, then braid a long string of them into a whip, swung from a distance would curl around the vampire and have the same result. How thick did it have to be? Did the silver immobilize it completely? Could it still move and possibly break the chains? All of it was speculation.

Not knowing the answers to these questions, the chief decided that two of his men skilled in small-arms use, and in-close fighting, would volunteer to bait the trap, rather than risk our amateur asses in a fight we weren't prepared for.

Lexi was furious, "We can do it, we're not children," he lamented, "I want to stake one of those bastards from hell."

He stalked away seething. The one most pleased with this decision was Dad,

"Don't tell Lexi I said it, but thank God you two aren't going to risk your lives, with me watching, I'd go mad. Carl I don't think Lexi has ever been in a fight, he always talks his way out of trouble, that's not going to work here."

"He thought as I did, we were the obvious bait," I said, "I never entertained the idea of asking someone else to do it, it just seemed our duty because we started this."

"You did not start this." Dad said forcefully, "Those creatures started it, if you and Lexi disturbed their nest; it was to help some good people. You fanned the flames, but the fire was there burning beneath, at least it's out in the open now, and the government is coming to the rescue."

I went to find Lexi; he was sitting on the band shell looking dejected.

"The chief is right," I said as I put my arm around his shoulders, "Were lovers not fighters."

He gave me his grin and squeezed my hand, "You always know how to make me feel better, but I'm still pissed off."

"I told Dad that it seemed we were the logical bait, like it's our duty, he didn't take that too kindly. He thinks we just stirred a pot, simmering for a long time. We can't blame ourselves for this, we didn't make the mess, we're just trying to clean it up."

The chief walked to the band shell, his hands jammed into his pockets as if he were mad at the world,

"I'm sorry Lexi, with our limited knowledge it was the best thing to do. My men are experienced shooters; they've had training to react fast. I have to give you credit for your courage, most guys your age would only do that to impress a girl they wanted."

He hesitated for a few seconds then asked, "Are you two gay?" He was embarrassed for asking, but it must have been on his mind.

"Yes chief, we are," Lexi proudly stated, "We're lovers, and we're going to marry in New York later this year."

"It's not that you're obviously gay," the chief struggled for words, "You're always together, I've never seen one of you without the other very close. I don't have a problem with you being whatever you want to be, it's just that you blow all the stereotypes to hell."

"The two of you act like testosterone overloaded teenagers, jumping in the river, wanting to fight a vampire, exploring in places that could get you killed, what kind of gay guys are you?"

The last part he said with a big grin on his face, and everything went back to normal.

Shortly after 12-noon the two choppers set down on our little park, the villagers standing by like old hands at this, the second time these monsters landed here after all, the novelty had already worn off.

The choppers were full of equipment and more than 40-men. Cavers whose profession was exploring caves, (spelunkers are amateur explorers) and cartographers with their laptops and shotguns?

A caver explained the process called Impulse Response, several shots are fired in the direction they want to map, the echoes coming back are picked up by microphones, fed into the computer program, and there it is, every cubby hole, every crevice, and every passageway.

Basically, the sound creates echoes of different wavelengths. The shorter wavelengths come back faster, which indicates width. The longer wavelengths, indicate a narrower passage, and take longer to get picked up by the microphone, clear as mud isn't it?

It takes 1-day to do what used to take weeks, this mapping should be done today, but by tomorrow for sure, which was good news. Now we would know the direct route to the castle via the underground tunnels.

Lexi found Dvorak giving instructions to the new members of his swat team; he handed them to his second and came to tell us about his trouble finding silver chains. He persevered, and bought a large box of them from a decrepit warehouse that had seen better days.

I presumed that meant they were cheap. Hundreds of chains were in the box, each 1-meter long, 39-inches. Lexi and I looked at all the chains, then at each other, and cracked up as, as we called the chief.

"What are you laughing at?" he asked, looking into the box, "What the hell are we going to do with that?"

"That's what we were laughing at," I said, "I haven't got a clue what to do with them." We cracked up again. "Show them to Tomas he may have an idea."

Lexi picked up the box and almost fell over,

"Damn things are heavy," he grunted as he hefted it to his shoulder, "Make a mesh with these you'll need two men just to carry it."

Tomas knew immediately what to do when we told him about the mesh, weaving was a way of life in the mountains. He cleared the top of the bar, and joined two chains, laid them on the bar, and joined two more, laying it beside the other chain; we saw what he was doing, and started joining pairs of chain.

He soon had a mess of them all laying in the same direction, each a quarter of an inch from the other, one meter-wide. Two chains together made the length of this mesh more than six-feet. We lifted chains for Tomas to go under and over the 6-footers, weaving as if he did this for a living.

In no time we had a chain mail blanket, 39-inches-wide, and 78-inches-long, we didn't even use half the chains, and it wasn't all that heavy.

"How about making a few ropes of the rest of them?" Lexi suggested, "If we take it alive we won't have to stake it right there."

"Why do you want to keep it alive?" the chief asked, "If it got loose, It could kill someone again. I say stake it."

"Me too," I agreed, "But maybe we should make some rope anyway, we could block off exits with it."

"Anybody know how to braid?" Lexi asked.

Tomas to the rescue, we joined the chains together, three long, Tomas took three of them, fastened them together at one end, and handed it to me. I held it while he braided the three together; it made a fairly thick rope.

We made a dozen of them, and still had chains leftover. We surprised Sergeant Dvorak at how rapidly we had made our vampire traps, he had been skeptical about using these flimsy chains to immobilize a vampire who had superhuman strength. As a precaution we distributed the remaining chains to the members of our group, it might help if attacked.

Several stakes of ash were fashioned; according to Tomas the best wood to use next to rosewood-none was available, we went with ash. Prepared to meet the devil we left for the waterfall.

Dvorak split the squad in two, ten experienced men and five new men in each group, we headed for the cavern with one group, and the security guards. Dvorak took the other group and the cavers to the castle. The strategy was to give it, or them, no place to run.

Dvorak's second, briefed the men in the lower-level main chamber, the object was to drive the creature into the chamber where a guard would be acting as bait. When it showed, the silver blanket would drop on it from above; the other man waiting out of sight with the bait would drive a stake in its heart, and have it finished. Ever heard the saying 'The best laid plans of mice and men'?

The police started their sweep through the tunnels, making a racket to wake an army, going slowly to give the creature a chance to exit whatever chamber it was in. It worked as we planned, we heard the creature long before we saw it, keening as if it were in distress, maybe it had a premonition of death.

The bait was sighted and the creature lunged for him with unbelievable speed. The mesh blanket fell, hit its back, then fell to the floor, only making it howl, it didn't slow at all. It reached the guard/bait in a split-second, reaching for his throat he grabbed the silver chain around the guards neck, his hand flew up, and it howled louder, enraged now, and being burned.

The other guard feared shooting, possibly killing the guard under attack, the sniper didn't have a clear shot either; it must have been providence that saved the day. The guard had his weapon pointed at the creature when it lunged at him knocking him backward, as he fell he fired and hit the creature in the stomach-enough to stop it.

With the guard out of the way, several shots rang out and the creature went down, the second guard/bait tried to push the stake through the leathery skin and ribs, it wouldn't go through, Lexi picked up a large rock, ran to the guard holding the stake he pounded it, driving it into the creature's heart.

In every vampire movie, when a vampire dies his body goes up in smoke. This one just shriveled, looking not even half the menace it had been. Lexi got to kill a vampire, he was ecstatic,

"One down, two to go," he yelled, "We did it."

The chief was as happy as Lexi; he slapped him on the back and congratulated him,

"You did it kid you bagged yourself a vampire, too bad you couldn't have it stuffed and mounted on the wall, as if anyone would want to look at that horror."

Lexi came to me and gave me a hug whispering in my ear, "We did it lover."

We put the remains in a body bag with two of the silver ropes around it, no chance of it coming back this time; it was going to stay dead. The cavern felt different somehow, cleaner, maybe evil is tangible more than we know, and with it gone that fact was discernible.

The police did another sweep through the tunnels, they found nothing. It seemed as though everyone felt the difference, the somber pall hanging over us had disappeared.

We met with the other team at dinner time at the inn. They too had a somewhat successful afternoon, not only mapping more than half the cave system, but the cavers also found an empty coffin with dirt in it, a sign that a vampire had been using it during the day.

Dad was with the cavers, and when they found the coffin he suggested we leave some silver in it, just in case. The cartographer estimated the coffin to be almost directly below the ruins, no reading indicating a way up in that location. The next day would tell them whether there was an entrance to the ruined cellars.

The mood that night at the inn was reminiscent of the first night Lexi and I had spent there, villagers came and went more relaxed than we had ever seen them, they could feel it too, the absence of the pall hanging over the village.

With one creature dead, and one loose in Olomouc, left Vlad to be dealt with, but where was he? If the mere presence of these things casts such darkness and gloom over the entire surrounding area, why was it absent now?

Vlad was still somewhere up here, we're sure he is the master the assassins spoke so reverently of. I found Tomas relaxing with a beer after preparing dinner for so many people.

"Tomas, does any other village have problems similar to the ones you people have had?" Lexi asked him.

Lexi translated, and got the idea where I was taking the questions, right away.

"All have had the same crimes committed," He replied, "But they don't have the cavern behind the waterfall, and the castle, it was worse here, but they also lost family members to the evil ones."

"Is there any pattern to the crimes, like one here on Monday, one in another village on Tuesday, a third in a different village on Wednesday?"

"Quite often it happens like that, what are you thinking?"

"Do you think there's a location Vlad could hide out near one of the other villages?"

"Many such places exist in these mountains," Tomas replied, "I would have to ask people from those villages."

"You know how the evil feels, we could feel it in the cavern, we could feel it in the caves under the castle, have you ever heard someone from another village say he felt the evil?"

"It's spoken of everywhere in the valley, we don't want to know, truth be told. I see where you are going with this, you are a clever man Carl, I hope clever enough to outsmart the evil one."

"I will inquire about that to our villagers, then go to the next village and the next; most people in the neighboring villages are in some way related to people here. If we do the asking it will be faster, and they will be more open with us."

"Can you start the process tonight, so we can have some idea by tomorrow at this time?" I asked him, "It can't wait, we have to know if he operates out of multiple hideouts. It might take the battalion that the PM mentioned. This Vlad is indeed cunning; he would have to be to last for more than 550-years."

"The way you describe it makes me feel like we have not been doing our duty to get the monster and kill him." Tomas said ruefully.

"You didn't have access to the records in Olomouc, I saw similar crimes in other villages, but the records were poorly kept, and they weren't always dated, so I only went with this village. Then the demons from hell were gone, so was the feeling."

"As on May Day there was joy, and no bad feeling, they were elsewhere. Vlad is not here, nor is the bad feeling, put them together and you see the theory that he has other places to hide."

"That makes me feel a little better, but we were so in fear of him we didn't even try."

"Don't beat yourself up Tomas, with the constable and the bullies protecting him, you were at a great disadvantage, together we're going to make this alright."

Lexi had been asking Tomas the questions, and translating the answers without interjecting anything of his own, now he was looking at me with the most loving smile I've ever seen, I thought he was going to kiss me, not that I would have minded. Instead, he just said,

"That was awesome."

Tomas cornered some village men, and got them to start the process; they showed instant understanding of what we were looking for.

We weren't worried that the chief would hear us romping on the bed; Lexi had asked me if I minded that he was so quick to tell the chief we were gay,

"I've been called a faggot all my life; do you think you telling the chief would bother me?"

"I'm so proud to be your lover I don't care who knows," he said with defiance, "I was such a coward when I first met you, we shook hands, and I got a shock that went through my whole body, I knew what it was, I was attracted to you before you even talked to me. I saw you when I walked out the door, and thought you were the most handsome man I'd ever seen."

"Your sign made me think the gods were smiling on me by sending you looking for me. Then I got scared, it took me 5-months to admit that I wanted you as my lover, no matter what the consequences."

"I tried to make you believe I was homophobic, I wasn't. I had a gay experience my second-year in college, it was on and off for a year. I was miserable, afraid of being outed, knowing there was no love involved, and helpless to do anything about it. I ended it, but he continued to try to get me to go with him, and did so up to my last day in college."

"His friends were all the epitome of the accepted view most people have of gays, I couldn't live like that. I may be gay, but I'm a man, not a female in a man's body, so I pretended to be homophobic, it kept the fags off me, but I was still miserable. Then you came into my life, you don't know what a catch you are, you're talented, smart, good looking, got a body to die for, and you're kind. Did I leave anything out?"

"Yes, I got you, and that's all that counts, you have all those attributes too, it doesn't matter as long as we have each other. I love you, I have from the instant you said I'm Alexi Duburk"

The loving was particularly good that night, our hearts had been laid bare, there would never be a question whether it was love at first sight, we had just confessed to that fact.

Before we went to the caves under the castle we made a stop at the waterfall to check out the caverns, they were as we left them the day before. The smell of animal was replaced with a slightly sweet smell; I made a mental note to mention it to the geologist when he returned in a few days with his report.

CHAPTER 18

MAPPING THE CASTLE CAVERNS & THE 2ND KILL

Within a half-hour we left for the castle. Locating the cavers and police was easy; the place was a bedlam with gunshots echoing throughout the cave system. Microphones amplifying the echoes, police shouting orders, and Dad standing by a computer looking as if he weren't hearing anything out of the ordinary, wrapped up in the program.

The caves were beautiful, stalagmites rising from the floor in places 10 to 12-foot high. Some were conical, some resembling a test tube boiling over, some smooth, some ribbed, some twisted in spirals, all different sizes and colors.

The main attraction, though, were the stalactites, glittering in the bright lights, akin to huge icicles hanging from eaves, except these were gigantic, some almost touching the floor of the cave, they, as were the stalagmites, of all shapes and colors breathtaking reds, blues, greens, yellows, and oranges, to mention a few.

One huge stalactite looked like a waterfall, but brilliant royal blue with green and red streaks, my head was on a swivel, where to look next?

Lexi took me by the arm, "Are you thinking what I'm thinking?"

"You bet, this is too nice to seal up, what a tourist attraction this will make, and the added benefit of being below Dracula's Castle."

Dad saw us and came to talk to us, "Beautiful isn't it? You're already incorporating this into the area economic expansion, aren't you?"

We laughed, he's good, maybe he does read minds, then again, so does his son; at least he seems to read mine.

"What were you studying so intently over there?" I inquired, "Is the program so interesting?"

"It's amazing in a matter of minutes, the echoes draw out the exact perimeters of the cavern, tunnels, niches, bumps, hidden turns, and any other measurable feature. You can watch it reveal the chamber inch by inch, it's fascinating. They're just moving past the coffin area, they told me they'd be finished by noon."

Shouting and running police grabbed our attention rather forcefully. We moved toward the shouting, Sergeant Dvorak, was issuing orders for his swat teams to get in position for a possible assault.

The impulse response program had found a stairway going up, still under the castle ruins. Sgt. Dvorak wanted to play it safe, which was his directive. We got there just as the first of the swat team disappeared up the stairway, assault rifles at the ready. No shooting, no shouting, just a silence that spread throughout the cave.

Several minutes went by with no sound from above; people still in the cave were getting as restive as a herd of water buffalo suspecting a lion was nearby. Suddenly a figure appeared on the stairs, a sigh of relief, it was Sergeant Dvorak.

"Everything is okay folks there's no one there, Lexi could you, and Carl come up here?"

We made our way to the stairs, feeling a little apprehensive we climbed the stairs to a fairly large room, not a cave, part of the castle's sublevels. A doorway led out of the room to a corridor, we could see lights and hear voices, but otherwise no indication of vampire activity.

We entered a room that could only be called an anteroom to the king's chamber. Several coffins were set on either side of huge double doors that stood open to reveal a sumptuously furnished bedroom, except there was no bed, just an elaborately carved coffin with the lid closed.

Lexi asked the question on both our minds, "Is it occupied?" pointing to the coffin. "Should I get a stake?"

"No," Sgt. Dvorak said, "The lid won't stay up, we opened it very carefully."

The whole suite had a surreal look, sealed underground for centuries it still looked like a display in a museum. Maybe it was maintained by mind controlled bullies, goons, slaves, or who knows what. However, this suite was cleaned and dusted regularly; the collapsing walls would have pumped a ton of dust in here. No doubt was in my mind, this place was still being used.

The sergeant indicated we follow him; we left the suite and continued down the corridor, more suites, not as lavish, but still not your average mausoleums. These suites were not maintained, and had dust at least 1-inch deep everywhere. This must have been the daytime resting place of the nobility Vlad had with him, and it confirmed that the royal suite had been recently occupied. The corridor ended with a pile of rubble possibly the castle walls, which collapsed into the cellars.

With the entrance in the forest via the cave and through the labyrinth, his lair was well protected, until impulse response was invented. Vlad was found out, we had much more information in 2-days than in the past 300-years, we had Vlad on the run.

We photographed the rooms and corridors, including stairs and blocked passages with special attention to the 'Royal Suite' and its cleanliness. While the cavers were finishing, Lexi and I took pictures of the extraordinary formations in the cave, we planned to show them to the PM, and get his blessing for a governmental study to open the caves to the public.

The cavers finished their exploration and Impulse response program without finding any other passages or exits, on, or under the plateau. Only one way to get into Vlad's 'bedroom', and that way was known to us, we would riddled it with traps, for slaves, and for him.

First we needed to install cameras to know what we were dealing with, and devise some clever ways to activate the traps. The creature in Olomouc also needed elimination, a call to the Minister of Justice the day before gave no news of progress in its capture.

The report on the other one here, being dead was received with rejoicing; the officials were beginning to doubt if they could be killed. The minister instructed Sergeant Dvorak to call back today with a progress report on the mapping of the caverns.

Outside the entrance cave, Dvorak checked his cell phone for messages, and there were several, all from the same number. He called the number; the operator at the government building was trying to reach him for the Minster of Justice.

She transferred him through to the official's office. The news was devastating, the creature had killed again. It had gotten into the cellar of a commercial building through the storm drain. The pipe had been checked earlier, but being only 12-inches in diameter it was thought to be too small for the creature to fit into.

The exterior doors were of steel, and securely locked from the outside. A maintenance worker went into the cellar for supplies, was slain, and drained of his blood. Late this morning, workers noticed the door was unlocked and went to see whether someone was down there, they found the body of the worker, but didn't see the creature. They reported the grating over the storm drain was gone, and the place reeked of animal feces.

The Minister ordered us all back to Olomouc immediately, there had to be an all-out hunt for the creature before this killing became public with an ensuing panic. The chief, his crew, Lexi, and I gathered all our vampire fighting gear together, went out to the choppers, and found them crowded already with the cavers and police. Dvorak called for another chopper, and was told to take the cavers off the helicopter; another was dispatched as they spoke.

A few cavers were disgruntled, but they understood from our manner that something was up. Another half-hour flight and we were back in Olomouc. A captain of the Federal Police force met us and escorted us to a briefing already in progress.

On a large display-board was a layout of the city's storm drains, with a large red X denoting where the killing had taken place. Fortunately, the storm drains didn't connect with every building.

Someone had been busy; all the likely buildings where it could hide were listed with address and phone number. The only advantage we had was that it was still daylight so it would have to remain holed up somewhere.

A young police officer spoke up, "Do we know all the outlets of the storm drains? If we had that information, we could block the drains and flood them. It would save time, better than going to each building on the layout connected to the drain system."

Lexi jumped into the fray, "That would flood the building too, but the idea is good, except instead of flooding the system with water we use silver oxide in the drain of each building we search," pointing to the storm drain layout that showed cleanouts every second building, he said, "One man can go from cleanout to cleanout, and pour some into each, if the creature encounters it believe me we will know, the silver burns them and it will screech like a banshee."

"And where are we going to get silver oxide? The officer sneeringly asked.

"I just happen to have a couple of gallons of the stuff on hand; you never know when you're going to meet a vampire." Lexi sarcastically replied.

Chuckles went around the room; the Minister rapped the table,

"We are working together here. If you have an idea, let's hear it, if it can be improved on, let's hear that too. Lexi, did you bring the silver oxide with you?"

"Yes sir, we brought everything we have. My mother suggested silver fulminate, but we couldn't find anyone to mix it for us, do you have a chemist who would make some?"

"Silver fulminate is very unstable isn't it?"

"In large quantities yes it is. It's used in very small amounts in children's party noise makers; we wanted some mixed that wouldn't be lethal to us, but deadly to the creature."

The Minister shook his head and smiled, "The Prime Minister was right, you two know more about vampires than any of us. I'll pull some strings and see if we can get some fast."

The conversation then focused on the creature's ability to fit is such a small pipe. The videos we had were reviewed again, it didn't have much body mass, and its shoulders wouldn't be a problem.

The young officer, somewhat chastened, suggested,

"Maybe it stretches its arms over its head, and pulls itself along, how else could it move if its arm were at its side?"

Before Lexi could reply to him, I said, "You're very observant, that would have to be its method of moving, and makes it very vulnerable, it can only go in one direction. From the layout can anyone see an obvious way we can use this to our advantage? Are the cleanouts large enough for it to turn around?"

Another officer answered, "We checked a few of them this morning, they're the same size as the actual drains."

I pointed to a cleanout that had two lines coming into the main line, at right angles.

"Do you think it would be able to navigate a right turn in a small space like that?"

The officer looked at the chart for a minute,

"I don't see how it could manage to get its hips into the main line."

"I thought the same thing," I said, "Even if it's double jointed it wouldn't work. Logically then, it has to go straight ahead when it gets to the cleanout. Which means it may be in this building now."

I pointed to the building across the street from where the killing took place, Lexi clapped his hands,

"You're a regular Sherlock Holmes Carl, has anyone checked the adjacent buildings?"

The Minister raised his hand for quiet,

"We only found the body a couple of hours ago, we didn't want to risk the men until they were all briefed, and we had determined what our strategy will be. Let me recap; considering the way we think it moves in the drainpipes, it can only go forward, and can't negotiate a 90-degree turn. If it leaves the building the way it went in, it can only go across the main line to the drain from the building across the street, everyone see that?"

"Now that it's across the street it can turn around, but can only go back to the building it just left. Assuming it's intelligent enough to realize that it's trapped, it will attempt to escape by leaving the building the normal way, which it can't do until dark. Now we need a strategy to get the creature. Anyone?"

Sergeant Dvorak took control, "The chief of security the boys hired and I have been analyzing the situation, we feel a ploy similar to the one used to kill the other creature is the only way.

This thing is fast, it moves with incredible speed, normal methods of apprehension won't work, we almost lost one of the guards because of the speed at which the thing attacked, a silver chain saved his life."

"No more close calls, we're going to make it do things our way. Instead of reacting to it, it will have to react to us, for instance; not being able to back up gives us a major advantage, we can direct it where we want it to go."

"Someone asked me if it can't make a 90-degree turn in the pipe, how did it get in the building drain from the cleanout? The chief and I think it could get around that turn because its weight was pushing it down and forward, it wouldn't have that needed push if the turn is on the same level."

"Right now if it's in the building across the street, the only place he can go is back to the killing site. We leave it where it is for now, and set a trap in the other building. A swat team assaults the building, and it's forced to retreat into the drain, once it leaves that location we pour silver oxide into the cleanout to prevent it using the storm drains at all."

"When it comes back up into the first building, we ambush it with the silver-chain-mail, silver rope, and wooden stakes."

"The speed at which the thing can move is our main concern; in the cavern the chain mail was dropped the second the thing came through the tunnel entrance, and it only grazed its back, we need to slow it." the chief added.

"If we laid the ropes out around the drain wouldn't that slow it?" I asked.

"If it touches them before it's completely out of the drain, it'll just slide back into the pipe, and be a problem getting it out." chief responded.

"Then we lay the ropes starting at a 2-foot radius from the drain, once it steps on just one of them will give it pause, multiple ropes for it pass, has to have the desired result," I responded, "The chain mail hanging over the drain would find an easier target too."

"We'll know better the exact plan once we get in the crime-scene basement," Dvorak pronounced, "Second, divide the men into 2-teams, we strike across the street after we set up in the target area."

"Lexi, bring your silver oxide, and make sure you have a communication device on you, we'll have to wait until it starts to come in the target area before we dump the poison, its too bad we can't track it to know exactly when it passes the cleanout."

"We can Sergeant," Lexi said, "With one of the spy cams, we only need to drill a tiny hole in the lid of the drain cleanout, and we can see it as it goes by, then notify you that it's on its way."

"You don't need to drill a hole," the officer who spoke earlier announced, "Holes are in it already for venting the lines, this is not a sewer line, there's no gases."

"Excellent," Sgt. Dvorak said, "That will allow us a few minute to get into position. Move out, we'll meet at the target."

The target Sergeant Dvorak was referring to was only a few blocks from the government buildings where the morgue was located, a commercial, and warehouse district, thankfully not residential.

We came in like an invasion; the few employees of the buildings we were targeting were evacuated, and stood around watching from a block away, held back by police barricades and a handful of officers.

Workers from other buildings were hanging out of windows trying to see what was going on, there was no way this could stay secret.

No sooner did I have that thought, when two TV camera crews showed up at the barricade demanding to film whatever was happening. The prediction of a circus was about to come true, Sergeant Dvorak stayed calm, but worried this would escalate.

Lexi talked to him for a minute and the tension relaxed. I asked him what he said,

"I told him to keep all the police inside the buildings; I would wait outside with the silver oxide until they have rousted it. Only then will I put the camera in the hole of the drain cleanout, you are going to have the receiver, when you see it go past the camera, signal Dvorak in the basement, and I'll hear it too. I remove the lid, pour some solution in, close it and we go to the cellar. Nothing for them to film, when we come out the thing will be in a body bag."

"Assuming everything goes as planned?" I asked. Lexi nodded, he wasn't as confident as his words sounded.

The time for action arrived, the swat team in position in building number two, were told to proceed. By the noise they were making I thought the watchers at the end of the block could hear, but it was from the open mike in the other cellar that was getting a transmission from the swat team. Muffled gunfire came from the basement and cursing, it was not retreating down the drain, the creature ran into another part of the cellar.

A warren of rooms made up of a series of storage bins, some locked some with no doors at all, only 50% at most occupied. The police knew the storage bins were there and the maze they created, with the creature in the basement there had been no way to develop a plan to force it in any particular direction.

Now we had a problem, every officer on the swat team was in jeopardy, the tools to subdue it, and kill it were across the street.

Lexi, always on the ball picked up the lid of the drain and poured half the solution in the cleanout, replaced the lid, and motioned me to follow him. We proceeded to the entrance of the building currently under siege, before we could enter; a police car came screaming down the street.

The driver jumped out and opened the passenger door, on the seat was a skeet thrower and a box with 2-dozen clay skeet traps. In the center of each was a foil packet taped securely to the disk.

"Silver fulminate," the driver said, "You requested this? I was told to tell you, handle with care."

Lexi was on the radio in a flash,

"Sergeant, we're going to take it out in the other building, the Minister just had the silver fulminate delivered. Bring everything here, there's nothing we can do about the press, they'll have only pictures of a swat team. I poured the silver oxide into the cleanout so it can't leave this building; we're in for a long siege."

The driver helped us get the thrower, and the skeet traps into the building lobby, the sergeant and the swat team were already heading across the street carrying the mesh, ropes, and stakes concealed by the body bag. Dvorak dismissed the driver, and we headed for the basement.

The Sergeant's second-in-command was no beginner, he had half the perimeter of the basement under the gun, you might say. Fifteen police officers armed with assault rifles formed a line that would prevent the creature from escaping the building, or going back down the drain.

They were instructed not to fire their guns unless they had a clear shot to the head, or body. God knows what was stored in those bins, and a ricocheting bullet could have dire consequences for us all, and the building.

Sergeant Dvorak and Lexi had a little parley, then explained what we were going to do. As the chief had strategized, we had to direct it, not react to it, so using the silver ropes we prevented it from going back into the storm drain. Simultaneously in 2-man teams we sealed one corridor after another with the silver rope, one man to fasten the rope, and one at the ready with his assault rifle.

Lexi had found a rolling table/cart in an open bin, and used it to set up the skeet thrower; he rolled it to the nearest corridor and fired. It exploded on contact with the wall at the end of the corridor. Brilliant yellow and silver was all anyone could see, powerful stuff this fulminate. Dvorak was pleased it worked so well, but we had to be careful where the traps exploded.

Satisfied with the performance of the skeet thrower, we went into a huddle to figure out how best to use it. Dvorak's second drew us a picture of the basement layout on the floor as best he could figure where the corridors started and ended, it wasn't a large space, just haphazardly laid out.

I suggested taking the silver oxide spray and go with a couple of guards armed with silver bullets, we could circle the basement clockwise; closing off corridors with the ropes as we went, Lexi could push his cart counterclockwise, closing off corridors as they progressed.

Lexi asked me to fire the aerosol container to see what reach it had. Pointing the nozzle slightly up I let a stream of liquid fly down the corridor, It traveled more than 15-feet, not far enough in his estimation, I knew he was worried the thing would get too close, and I would be its target.

"A rifle with silver bullets in them will be on either side of me, if the spray doesn't reach its mark their bullets will. Stop worrying, we have to eliminate this monster."

"Then go slowly and listen for that keening sound."

We crept down the corridor, checking doors that weren't padlocked, I stayed back as each door was opened, these guys were trained in this kind of search, and didn't take any chances they weren't prepared to handle.

Our lead was almost at the end of the outside corridor when one of the traps exploded around the corner, the screeching was earsplitting in this enclosed space, we were already on high alert, but it still went up a notch or two.

We stopped, and crouched, anticipating its appearance around the corner. It didn't happen. We move again, to the corner there was nothing there, another corridor opened a few feet from the corner, going toward the center of the basement.

The corridor behind us was blocked off, and we started toward the one just revealed, there was nothing in the corridor, but there were several doors hanging open.

Lexi called on the radio and asked my position, I explained approximately where we were, there was a corridor heading back toward where we started. He thought the best way to make it go where we want it to go was to block off that avenue and continue forward. We complied and went forward.

Another trap exploded, this time very close, something was moving our way, again we prepared for a fight, another trap exploded followed be screams of pain? Anger? Disconcerting to hear, almost as bad as seeing the creature. We continued forward expecting any second to see it.

We approached the turn at the end of the corridor, with trepidation. The screams had come from this direction, we had no inkling of what to expect, the three of us turned the corner together.

The creature was on its knees in front of us no more than 10-feet away; it was badly wounded by the silver fulminate. A wounded creature can be more dangerous than ever, my trigger finger was definitely itchy, the moment I saw it I sprayed a long shot of the oxide into its eyes, the screeching was worse than before.

Both guards shot it simultaneously as it started to rise, it fell backward, and I jumped to put the stake in its heart. I held the stake while a guard hammered the stake home with the butt of his weapon. The second creature was dead. Crisis averted.

CHAPTER 19

OPENING UP TO THE PM

The Prime Minister was ebullient as he listened to our report of the slaying of the second monster.

"I wish I could give you boys a medal and honor you in public the way you deserve. We can't do that for reasons you're well acquainted with, but be assured your service will not go unnoticed or unrewarded."

"We are not looking for recognition or reward, any reward should go to the people of River Town, and neighboring villages, they have suffered long enough. Two terrors are eliminated, but the main one still exists."

"We intend to follow through with this, there are several leads we're pursuing, we think he has multiple lairs, one in different villages, and helpers in each village also. If you have the time, we have some pictures we would like to show you."

The PM looked through the pictures we took of the royal suite, and the other suites, he picked it up immediately and asked, "Why don't the first pictures show an inch of dust like the others? Am I missing something?"

"Somebody is cleaning it for him, probably under his mind control," Lexi said, "We installed spy cameras to see who comes there when no one else seems to know that an entrance to the caverns exists."

"These rooms are underground?" The PM asked, "If this is the cellars of the castle, what did the upper floors look like? How extensive was the destruction?"

"These rooms were the daytime retreats of Vlad and his nobles. We measured the ruins, and figure it was about 17,000-square-feet per floor, by the look of the rubble in the basements it was more than 1-floor, it's hard to tell, most was cleared away when they made it a tourist attraction 35-years ago." Lexi explained,

"We have some more pictures we'd like you look at, they are of the area below the castle," Lexi held out the photographs of the beautiful colors of the caverns, "We need to get your blessing on a matter of great economic impact to this area"

The PM took the pictures and gaped, "These are the caverns below Dracula's castle?"

"They are, and they don't do justice to the entire cave system, it's extensive and at every turn there's another marvel of nature's beauty. We don't want you to think we are opportunists, coming here to take advantage of a region, its people, or its natural resources."

"I wouldn't disclose this to anyone, ever, but Carl and I have agreed that you at least, have to know about us. We are not poor tourists, our combined wealth is well over a billion dollars, if you want conformation it will be provided by our lawyers in New York."

"We try to be ordinary people and help where we can. Please keep this information confidential we have many people waiting to take advantage, it complicates matters."

"I'm speechless; not very many people in this corrupt world have a fraction of your ethics or kindness. I've known for several days now who you are, and how much you're worth, your honesty is refreshing, I am very much in awe of you two."

"I intend to make you national heroes, not now, but you will get the recognition you deserve. One day soon there will be equality in the marriage act, and I would be proud to do the honors."

"How do you know about us?" Lexi stammered, "Six months ago I didn't even know."

"It's my job to know with whom I am dealing, I have a very demanding job, there's an enemy around every corner waiting to take me down, like you have a vulture waiting for you. It will go no farther than this office, and I am the office. I wish I could proclaim it to the world, you are good people, and I will not do anything to harm you in any way."

"The answer to your question about opening the cavern to the public is a resounding yes, and I'll go an extra mile, let's partially rebuild the castle at the government's expense."

"Clean out the collapsed walls from the cellars, make the rooms you discovered under the castle part of a visitor's tour of Dracula's castle, will that have an economic affect Carl? Especially after you write one of your excellent travelogues?"

"You know I'm a writer?"

"I just told you it's my business to know, I've read your work, and it's like everything you do, way above average. These are my people too, and I do have empathy for their situation, we can't change it in the bright lights of the media, you know that, why else would you want me to keep your secret?"

A pair of very subdued vampire hunters left the PM's office, "What just happened Carl, does the whole world know about us?"

"I don't think so Lexi, I really don't think they care. I would like to know how he found out so much."

"Probably just a call to the government in Washington, and the FBI has a file on you in the blink of an eye, he's the head of a friendly nation, you think they don't co-operate that way? You're an American

National operating in his country, he has a right to know who you are, and what you're doing," Lexi pontificated,

"We have stirred up a mess here, it's not as if you're just a tourist, we were expecting him to trust us just because we told him we weren't crooks, you don't do that when people try to get money out of you."

"A good point, I know I'm not a crook, so its human nature to think everyone automatically accepts it as fact. Pretty naïve, isn't it?"

"I did the same thing Carl, when I was lying to myself, I felt no one thought differently, but Dad did. We're two innocent little puppies with a lot to learn."

The sergeant was waiting at the helicopter, "I stowed your gear for you, and we included the skeet shooter in case you have a run-in with Vlad. There's nothing we can do at this time in the mountains, if we try to help find locations where he might be hiding, it would upset the locals way out of proportion to the benefit you'd get."

"We're only a half-hour away if you need us, don't take unnecessary risks, if this Vlad survived for 500-years, he didn't do it by being stupid. The two we killed were more animal than human with animal cunning for self-preservation; they had no mental acuity to avoid capture."

"Vlad is another story; he's diabolically clever, and will try to outmaneuver you at every turn. He may also go on the offensive, watch for little things that don't seem to fit."

"Good luck guys, it's been a hell of a week." We shook hands and boarded the helicopter.

Dad, the mind reader cornered us the second we jumped down from the chopper,

"You put yourselves in harm's way again didn't you, the two of you have guilt written all over your faces; tell me the whole story, leave nothing out."

Lexi started by trying to minimize the risk we had taken, that 30-police were there with us mollified him a bit, but he still worried about the risks we were taking. The telling was much less dramatic than the actual event, he accepted it, hugged us, and threatened to use the leashes again.

"The geologist is on his way here, he called an hour or so ago, he'll be here in less than an hour. He wouldn't tell me what's in the report, but he said it looked good. Did you show the PM the pictures?" Dad inquired.

That animated Lexi, "You bet, and Dad he gave us permission to see if the place is safe, after Vlad is staked. The best part is he's going to have the castle partially rebuilt to make it look more like a 500-year-old ruin than a pile of rubble. Clean up the cellars and the rooms with the coffins, then have tours where there is something to see, not just stones."

"We told him about the money so he wouldn't think we were con artists, he said he already knew, he knows that Carl is a writer and he knows we're gay, he offered to marry us when the laws change to permit total equality, how would he know? Did you talk to him?"

"I would never discuss your private life with anyone except you two and your mother, I imagine he had a check run on both of you, You told him the first time we went to Olomouc that Carl is an American, and that you two had formed the Hydro Electric Foundation. For a Politian that's lot of information, and also a red flag. You went to New York one time, 10-years ago, do you suppose he thought you and Carl collaborated on the power station then?"

"He had you checked first, then Carl, he's most likely good at basic math, if Carl came here in December and by June you're living in a jointly owned condo, share a trust fund worth seven-hundred-fifty million dollars each, and are in each other's pocket as you put it, what other conclusion could he come to?"

A slightly less animated Lexi was defiant, "They can't give out information like that can they? What happened to the right of privacy? How many others now know these things?"

I had to calm my raging bull before he had a fit,

"Lexi, the PM wouldn't publish the fact that he had us investigated, or vetted as they say in the US, maybe his personal secretary knows, but that would be all, you need a lot of influence to get that kind of information so calm down."

"Dad's right he put two and two together, do we mind if he knows? He volunteered to marry us himself, I say we get married in NY and Prague, we'll be citizens of each other's country."

Lexi hugged me, and there was a tear in the corner of his eye, 'I love you' he whispered.

ABOUT THE AUTHOR

I am a retired contractor, 76 years old, This book has been in my head for years now, and since I retired, thought it the parfect time to put it on paper.

I was schooled in Canada, and had 2-years of Speech therapy studies. I don't believe this is a qualifier for authorship, but when I started the first book of the series, now 7-books, it just took on a life of its own.

due to the conten of the book one would naturally ask whether I'm gay, the answer is yes, I had 31-years with my life-mate before he succumbed to a respiratory ailment. During those years we raised 5-children, all happily married-I hope.

I became an American citizen years ago, and I'm still happy about that decision. I'm a political junkie, and follow the shenanigans of both parties, lately with great disappointment with the partisan bickering.

I've been an avid reader for many years, which gave me the courage to start writing, anybody who thinks it's easy, has never written a book. I write daily and walk 2 or 3-miles, I don't participate in sports. My life has been productive and fulfilling, I have no regrets except for the constant homophobia encountered at every turn. I try to portray my social conscience in a light of equality and fairness. As an athiest I strive to allow other's opinions to not inflame but learn from their rationalizations.

I currently live with my eldest son and his 7-year old daughter, the light of my life, in Phoenix, Arizona.